All She Wanted Was a Rider 3

By: Kellz Kimberly

Text **KKP** to **22828** for Updates, Spoilers, Giveaways, Announcements, & So Much More!!!!!

Previously in **All She Wanted Was a Rider**

Ryan

I didn't want to leave Harlem hanging, but the things Demetri whispered in my ear; I couldn't pass up. Once she was gone, Demetri led me to the guest room where he stayed. Without saying a word, he pushed me onto the bed. He went to work, taking off my sneakers and pulling my jeans off. I felt like a high school girl going to third base with the captain of the football team.

"I couldn't wait to get you alone again," he said, laying on top of me.

"You addicted to the kitty already?" I moaned. He was biting and sucking on my neck, getting my body all worked up.

"I just might, if you let me taste it," he whispered in my ear.

"Be my guest," I told him. Head was something I would never turn down. If he wanted to feast on my kitty, I would let him. There was no way I was turning that down.

He rubbed me through my panties, causing some friction. I was already wet, and he was just making it worse. The rubbing switched to him nibbling, and I was ready to bust. I kid you not, I could have sworn Demetri was trying to eat my panties. He nibbled on my clit like the thin laced fabric wasn't even there.

"Ahhhh," I moaned. I pushed his head away and wiggled out of my panties. He was teasing me and I wanted to feel his thick tongue, gliding across my clit.

"You ready?" he asked me.

I nodded my head yes. My body was anticipating whatever he was ready to give me. I closed my eyes, ready to enjoy the tongue lashing Demetri was about to give me. He blew on my clit and gently licked it. I could have sworn I felt something popping against it, but I wasn't sure.

Demetri slipped two fingers inside of me, twisting them in and out. My body trembled from the sensation he was giving me.

"Oh shit!" I yelled.

Demetri had latched on to my clit, and this time, I knew something was popping against it. At first, it felt uncomfortable, but after a while, it felt good. Whatever he was using to pop against my clit was driving me crazy. My clit was vibrating while he sucked on it.

"Mhmmmmm Ryan, this pussy good," he mumbled.

Demetri was doing his damn thing. His tongue assaulted my clit. Enzo had some good head, but he had nothing on Demetri. He slipped his fingers out just as his tongue did a lap around my clit, and then went down to my ass crack. I jumped from never having my ass crack licked.

"Relax bae, I got you. Lift up," he moaned. I relaxed my body and lifted up. Demetri took each ass cheek in his hands and went to work. I tried to think if I had shitted at all today because if I did, that would have been nasty.

"Yesssss," I hissed. Demetri's tongue waved in and out, causing me to reach heights of pleasure I never knew existed.

"Let that sticky, creamy stuff go," Demetri demanded.

I reached over, rubbing my clit. I was in pure bliss as both of us brought me to a new high. Demetri replaced his tongue with his finger, and that's when it was all over.

"Ahhhhhhhhh!" I screamed out.

My stomach cramped up as I exploded. Demetri used his tongue to catch everything I had to offer.

"Yessssssss, yessssss, yessssss!" I cried. I was literally in tears by the time Demetri finished licking me. I lay on the bed, unable to move. I felt paralyzed after the head he had just given me.

"You 'ight over there?" Demetri asked, stepping out of his basketball shorts. His dick stood at full attention and I didn't think I was ready for that.

"What was that you had in your mouth when you were sucking on my clit?" I needed to know if that was his mouth putting in all that work, or if he had help, because if it was all his mouth, then that nigga deserved a damn pussy eating award.

"It was pop rocks. You never had a nigga eat you out with pop rocks?" he asked like I was out of the loop.

"No."

"I got a few things to show you, but for now, let me teach you how to work this dick," he stroked himself and the sight alone brought my body to life.

"Lay down," I told him. I moved out of the way to give him enough space. I noticed the nigga didn't have a condom, and this time, that shit wasn't happening. I slipped up yesterday at the club, but I wouldn't slip up again.

"Where are your condoms?"

"In the drawer to your left," he answered, licking those thick lips.

I reached over and pulled out a box of magnum condoms, extra-large. *Makes sense*, I said to myself. I ripped one open and rolled it on, using my mouth. Enzo made me use condoms so much that I learned a few ways to put them on.

"Oh shit!" Demetri laughed.

"Shut up boy and watch me work. Hold your dick in place," I told him.

I squatted over his dick with my hand behind my head. I eased down, making sure I got all of him. I was still in a squatting position when I started bouncing my ass.

"Fuck! You doing it with no hands," Demetri moaned.

I wasn't going to pull out all my tricks, but I planned to show him a few. I rolled my body until I was using my knees to hold me up, placed my hands on his chest and whined my hips like I was dancing in the club. Demetri reached up to caress my breasts and toyed with my nipples. My nipples were my sensitive spot. As soon as Demetri touched them, I started leaking.

"Yeah, give daddy that gushy shit."

"Damn this dick feels good." I tilted my head back, fully enjoying everything Demetri had to offer. I was getting every inch of that dick, and even though it brought me pain, the pain heightened the pleasure.

"I done been around the world, I done kissed a lot of girls so I'm guessin' that it's true. Make me holla and I bet a million dollars don't nobody kiss it like you. Don't nobody kiss it like you, don't nobody kiss it like you, bang, bang, bang. Don't nobody kiss it like you, don't nobody kiss it like you."

Usher's song, "Good Kisser", played and I knew it was my phone. I was in the middle of getting some good dick and someone had the nerve to call me. I went to reach for the phone because it could have been Harlem calling for me, but before I could even reach it, Demetri reached over and snatched it up.

"Hello?" he said, answering the phone. I was still rocking my hips, trying to pay attention to who was on the phone.

"Yeah," Demetri said. I didn't know who he was talking to, but he had a smirk on his face. If he was going to entertain someone on my damn phone, then I would fuck his mind up. I used my hands to lift my body up. I stretched my legs out and popped back down on his dick in a split.

"FUCK!" he yelled out. I popped my ass in a split on his dick like I was trying to get them ones.

"Nah, she can't come to the phone right now," he said to whoever was on the phone. "Slow up ma," he told me.

"She's busy riding this dick!" he spat into the phone and hung up.

"Who the fuck was that on the phone?" I asked him. I stopped moving all together because I was getting pissed. Here I was, doing splits on the dick, and he was holding a conversation with someone on my fucking phone.

"She hung up," he said and placed my phone back on the nightstand.

"She? Was it Harlem?" I asked him.

"Nah, it was some chick from jail. I didn't know you rolled with bitches in the pen."

"What did she say?" I screamed. I picked my phone up and called the phone number back. I knew it was a waste of time, but I still wanted to try anyway.

"Ma calm down, the shit isn't all that serious. All she said was that Enzo was a bitch ass nigga, but we already knew that," Demetri shrugged.

"That was all she said?" I questioned, calming down a little.

"Oh, she said that nigga snitched on her or some shit."

"WHAT!" I yelled, hopping off his dick.

"Where the fuck are you going?" he asked, trying to grab me back.

"She's in jail for murder and I'm over here getting dicked down, instead of killing the nigga that fucking sent her there."

Demetri was trying to talk to me, but I was straight ignoring his ass. I needed to get the fuck out of here and find Isiah. This shit had to be some type of mistake. There was no way Enzo was a fucking snitch.

Chapter One: Alani

"Moore, you have a visitor!" the C.O. called out.

I got off my bunk and reluctantly walked over to my cell doors. I have been in this shit hole for only a day, and I was more than ready to get the fuck out. Jail damn sure wasn't for me, and once I got out, I had no plans on coming back. This shit was really for the birds. The C.O let me out and escorted me to a private room. I walked in and my lawyer was sitting at the table with a worried look on his face. I was hoping it didn't have anything to do with the bail hearing, because I needed that to come through. If I had to stay in my cell for one more day, I was sure to go crazy.

"How are they treating you in here Alani?" he asked once the C.O left out.

"They damn sure not waiting on me hand and foot. I'm holding up though. So wassup, I thought I wasn't going to see you until Monday?

"I came upon some information that couldn't wait until Monday. As I told you before, they don't have any evidence on you, but they do have something serious on you."

"Okay, so what is it?" My hands began to sweat as I waited for him to start speaking. He shuffled through a couple of files before placing one in front of me.

I looked down and sitting in front of me, clear as day, was a picture of Enzo getting in and out of a black Lincoln town car.

Anyone who was doing anything illegal already knew what that meant. Enzo was a snitch.

"The guy in the picture is the key witness in your case. He is supposed to testify against you on the murder of Khalil. Do you have any idea how he would know about the death of Khalil?"

"Nah," was all I was able to say. Shock wasn't even the word to express how I felt. Betrayed was more so the word. Enzo was like a brother to me, so to learn he betrayed me, hurt.

"Now is not the time to be tight lipped, Alani. If you know anything, now is the time to speak up."

"Do you really think if I knew something I wouldn't tell you? This is my life on the line here. I'm the one that will be facing twenty-four to life, not you or anyone else, but me. So if I did know something, best believe I would be singing like a canary," I told him. I wasn't lying either. I really didn't know anything that would connect Enzo to the murder. I didn't even know how he knew about the murder.

"Well, as far as bail, I'm more than certain they are going to deny it. I will still do my best in trying to get you out of here. In the meantime, don't say anything to anyone about what I told you. Let's just keep this between us for now."

"Okay."

The C.O. came back to take me to my cell. I laid on my bunk, thinking about how my life took a turn for the worst. I knew the risks I was taking by doing the things that I did, but I never thought I would get caught up. My team and I were too slick to get got. It took someone on the inside to get us hemmed up. I was worried, but at the same time, I wasn't. I saw it like this; if I eliminate the problem, then I would get off Scot-free. I just had to figure out how to get it done without Isiah and Ques finding out. The Feds were watching, and Isiah and Ques would be their main focus. I didn't want them trying to handle Enzo and wind up being caught up. Nah, this had to be handled without their knowledge. As soon as it was yard time, I was going to make that call to my girls because they were the only ones I trusted enough to handle this. If I was going to get out of here, then it was going to take the Lady Killers to get this done.

* * * *

"FUCK!" was all I heard when some nigga answered the phone. It wasn't a yell, but more like a moan.

"Who the hell is this? Matter of fact, never mind, can you put Ryan on the phone!" I was annoyed because it sounded like this nigga was fucking while I was on the phone.

"Nah, she can't come to the phone right now. Slow up ma." I let out a sigh of frustration because the nigga was really irking my soul.

"I don't care what she's busy doing, I need you to put her on the phone. Her ex is a fucking bitch nigga and he's the reason I'm in jail!" I barked. I got a couple of stares from the other inmates, but I didn't give a fuck.

"She busy ridin' this dick," he spat. I removed the phone from my ear and slammed it down. At that moment, I realized it could have only been one person on the phone.

Demetri, I said to myself, shaking my head. I couldn't believe this shit. Don't get me wrong, I was happy Ryan was getting her groove back, now just wasn't the time for her to be doing it.

"Inmate, do I need to bring you back to your cell?"

"No, I'm okay," I said.

I had to take a deep breath because Demetri had me hot. I waited a couple of minutes to call back, and this time, Ryan answered the phone.

"Alani! Oh my God, I'm so sorry about that," she said in one breath.

"Look Ryan, what I'm about to tell you can only be repeated to Harlem. I don't want the guys finding out, ight?" I didn't give her a chance to answer, I just kept talking.

"Enzo is a snitch; he is working with the DEA. I don't know why he thinks I killed ole boy, but he is the only thing stopping me from beating this case."

"You can't expect me not to tell the guys, Alani; this shit is important. Isiah and Ques will kill me if I hold something this important from them," Ryan stressed.

"You think I don't know how important this is. It's my life that's on the line. I don't want the guys involved, and I don't want them at any of my court dates."

"I don't see how you expect me to keep it from the guys, but okay Lani."

"Ryan, I'm serious. I don't want them to know shit. If they are in the dark, the better things will be."

"I said ok Lani, damn. How are you though? No bitch is trying to lick that cat, right?" she giggled.

"You already know I don't get down like that. So if someone tried, they wouldn't get far."

"I'm about to go talk to Harlem about what you told me."

"No, wait until tomorrow. It's kind of late, and I don't want Isiah being suspicious."

"Okay girl, I love you and keep your head up. I'll come visit you soon."

"I love you too, Ryan."

"Don't worry about nothing," Ryan told me before I hung up the phone.

I hoped like hell Ryan kept her word and didn't tell the guys. Isiah would be alright because he had Harlem, but I knew Ques was going to be fucked up about it. He was probably going to think I was trying to be tough and handle shit on my own. When in reality, I was doing this to protect him. The more I thought about it, the better I thought it would be for Ques to come visit me. In order for things to work out the way I had them planned, I needed to end things with Ques. I wasn't heartless, so ending it with a letter wasn't going to work. I needed to end things face to face. Hopefully when this whole thing was over, there will be no bad blood between me and Ques. I love him, and when you love someone, you will go to extreme lengths to protect them.

Chapter Two: Ryan

That shit Alani just told me surprised the shit out of me. I mean, Ciara did tell us that Enzo was not to be trusted, but she was an enemy in my eyes. I wasn't going to believe shit she said until she had proof. Alani on the other hand had proof. Her sitting in jail was proof enough. It hurt me that Enzo would do some shit like that to Alani. Alani, Isiah, and Enzo were like brothers and sisters. This shit was going to kill Isiah whenever he found out. I couldn't understand why Alani wanted to keep it from Ques and Isiah, but I was going to honor her wishes. First thing tomorrow, I was linking up with Harlem because we had to come up with a plan to take the nigga out. Damn, I had to take the nigga out. It could have been the love I once had for him, but just the thought of killing Enzo was pulling my heart strings. Tears started to fall from my eyes as I thought about all the bullshit that was happening. I had literally been sleeping with the enemy for years, and now I had to kill him. If that wasn't some bullshit, then I didn't know what was.

"You ight ma?" I forgot Demetri was in the room. I looked back at him, nodding my head. I gathered all my clothes off the floor and began putting them on. I had fun with Demetri, but I need to get my head in the game, and him being around wasn't helping it.

"Where you going ma? You leaving me already?" he asked.

"I need to get home."

"I thought you was fucking with me for the rest of the night?"

"Did you think I was really going to lay up in the house where your sister is?" I half laughed because he couldn't be serious. It was one thing to get it on here, but to actually spend the night, that was a different story.

"We don't have to stay here. I'll get us a room. I'm just trying to be next to you, Ryan. Is that too much to ask?" He came over to where I was standing, wrapping his arms around me. My body melted into his instantly. It was crazy, but Demetri and I had this deep connection that was unexplainable.

"Let me be here for you. I don't know what's going on, but I do know you need a shoulder to lean on. Let me be that for you," he whispered in my ear.

"I'm fine Demetri, trust me. The last dude I leaned on ended up doing me dirty. I don't want to go down that path again. I want to be able to handle things on my own." The strength I was telling Demetri I had, didn't exist. In fact, I needed someone to lean on because I was truly at my worse. I was just scared about taking it to that level with Demetri.

"Stop with the dumb shit. That's what's wrong with women," he spat, slightly pushing me away. He sat at the edge of the bed and glared into my eyes.

"Why when a nigga do a woman wrong, y'all want to think the next nigga is going to do you wrong too? I'm letting you know now, I'm not that type of dude. I don't have time to be cheating and shit like that because if I don't want you anymore, I will let your ass know and leave you wherever the hell you stand. I don't have time for the games. I just turned twenty-five, not twenty-one. If you can't handle a nigga that wants to get to know you and maybe build something with your annoying ass, then that's cool, you can step."

I was caught off guard by what Demetri just said to me. Demetri was saying all the right things to me, that's how it always starts. Niggas spit that game to get you, then when they get your ass, they want to start fucking up.

"I can handle anything that comes my way, believe that. There is more to me than the sex crazed cry baby that you have seen. If you coming with me, you might want to get dressed because I don't like waiting on people," I smirked.

"You have no choice but to wait because you gave your girl the keys to your car," he laughed.

"Shut the hell up and let's go," I sassed.

I laughed on the inside because he was right. I forgot about giving Harlem my car keys. I made a mental note to call her and tell her to drop my car off at my house. I watched Demetri get dressed with lust filled eyes. Demetri was fine, and just the sight of him had me ready to go another round.

"You can stop looking because you not getting any more for a minute. This thing we got going between us is going to be more than just sex. Now bring that ass on so I can see if you can cook."

"Don't nobody want you boy, move," I giggled. I pushed him out of the way and walked downstairs. Ciara was in the living room with one of her little friends talking. The conversation came to a halt when I walked past them, while Demetri held on to my belt loop.

"Heyyy Demetri," Ciara's friend sang.

"Ciara, I'm out. I'll call to check on you to make sure you're straight. Oh, and when I get back, we will be having a conversation," Demetri said, ignoring the other chick.

"Okay, but there is nothing to talk about."

"I think there is since Enzo isn't the baby's father," Demetri spat.

"Stop telling my business Demetri, damn," Ciara pouted.

"You should have been handling your business, then there wouldn't be anything to tell." He grabbed my hand, leading me out the door. For Demetri not to be a street nigga, he carried himself like one. His aura scream head nigga in charge. His attitude damn sure showed he was the nigga in charge.

"Plug your address in the GPS," he told me.

I did as I was told, typing in my address. After that, I leaned back in my chair, comparing and contrasting Demetri and Enzo. Enzo was a pretty boy for real. Everything about him was gorgeous, which was probably the reason why I fell for him. He was a pretty boy that all the girls wanted, but he chose me. Demetri on the other hand was rough and rugged, and I loved it. Enzo tried to come off hard, while with Demetri, it came naturally.

"This shit is crazy," I giggled to myself.

"What's crazy?" Demetri asked, looking at me from the corner of his eye.

"Nothing."

"Stop with that nothing shit. Now tell me what's crazy."

"I was comparing you and Enzo in my head and it's crazy how different y'all are."

"Maybe you're just tried of the usual."

"I guess," I shrugged.

"It's the truth and you just don't want to admit it, but that's cool though. You need anything from the supermarket or you straight?"

"Nah, my house stays stocked. I got everything I need. You might want to stop and get you some pajamas though."

"I'm straight. I keep basketball shorts and a t-shirt in my gym bag in the trunk."

"Oh okay," I told him.

We pulled up to my house and out of nowhere, I got nervous. My house was always clean, so that wasn't an issue. It was just I haven't had any dude in my house besides Enzo. This shit was crazy; Enzo was really my whole life. I stepped out of the car and walked the short distance to my building. I held the lobby door, waiting for Demetri to grab his gym bag.

"Let's go, a nigga hungry," he laughed, walking in the door.

"Then I guess you're cooking," I told him, unlocking my front door.

We walked in my apartment and Demetri started walking all around my place. I let him do him because I wasn't up for a tour. I went in the kitchen to see what I could whip up real quick. Since I had ground turkey in the fridge, I decided to make burgers. It was something simple and easy, and wouldn't take long. I pulled out everything I needed, placing it on the counter.

I went to my room to change out of these street clothes before I started cooking. I walked in my room and Demetri was lying in bed, knocked out. I looked at him, shaking my head. I had only left him alone for about five minutes and his ass was already sleep. Before I changed my clothes, I stopped and gazed at him. Demetri was different, but different was something that I felt I needed. I wasn't saying I was falling in love or anything, but Demetri had me all caught up. Hopefully he would catch me when I fell.

Chapter Three: Harlem

"The fuck you mean she don't want me at her bail hearing!" Isiah yelling like he had no damn sense, woke me up out of a peaceful sleep.

I tried rolling over and ignoring him yelling, but the more he talked, the louder he got. I decided to get out of bed because sleep was over for me. I checked my phone to see if I had any missed calls or texts. I had a missed call and text from Ryan. The text said for me to bring her car over to the house. The text was from yesterday night, so I paid it no mind. The call on the other hand was from this morning. I dialed her number as I walked in the bathroom. It was a Sunday, and all I wanted to do was sleep in since Monday was Alani's court date.

"Why didn't you bring me my car last night?"

"Good morning to you too," I laughed.

"I need you to come over to my house ASAP."

"Give me like an hour or two. Isiah is going off on the phone because Alani doesn't want him at her bail hearing. I know he's gonna want to talk about it."

"That's what I need to talk to you about."

"What the hell is going on?"

"Just get over here and I'll explain everything. Can't really say much right now," Ryan said. I caught the hint she was throwing my way.

"Okay, I'll be there in thirty."

I hung up the phone, used the bathroom, washed my face, and brushed my teeth. When I was done, I headed back into my bedroom to get dressed. Both of my feet weren't even in the bedroom before Isiah started throwing questions my way.

"You talked to Lani? Why don't she want me at her bail hearing tomorrow?"

"Isiah, you need to calm down. I didn't do anything to you, so you need to move around with all that misdirected anger."

"Look, my bad. I just know how close y'all are."

"If it makes you feel any better, I don't know why she doesn't want you there. I haven't even talked to her."

"She on that bullshit. Now isn't the time for her to be playing games." I watched him as he fell onto the bed, resting his head in his hands. I truly felt his pain, but there was really nothing I could say. I had no clue what was going on. I walked over to the bed, standing in front of him. Lifting his head up, I wrapped his arms around my waist and rested his head against my stomach.

"You know Alani doesn't make moves unless she's thought the situation through. I'm sure whatever reason she has for not wanting you there is a good one. You can't stress it because you got a business to run, and you don't know who is out there watching y'all."

"What would I do without you?" Isiah asked, looking up at me.

"I don't know, but it's a good thing we won't have to find out any time soon."

Isiah pulled me onto his lap, cupping the back of my neck and pulling me into a kiss. His hands dropped to my inner thigh. He began rubbing it and inching his hand closer to the real prize. I entertained the thought of Isiah being inside of me, but then Ryan telling me she needed to talk to me popped in my head.

"That will have to wait until later. I have to go bring Ryan her car."

"She can wait."

"Isiah, you can wait. Stop acting like a horny teenager." I got up and Isiah smacked my ass.

I smirked at him before I started getting dressed. Today was supposed to be my lazy day; getting all dolled up was out of the question. Sweats and a hoodie were going to be my attire for the day. Ryan better have something good to say when I get there. I had this feeling things were about to get worse than they already are. If push came to shove, I would lay my body on the line to see my family straight. For me, it was all about family. Family over everything.

* * * *

"Uh, why are you opening Ryan's door?" I asked staring at Demetri. He was in a pair of basketball shorts with no shirt.

"I don't have to answer any questions. You can either come inside or sit on the porch," he smirked, walking away from the door.

No this nigga didn't, I thought to myself. "Ryan!" I called out, walking in the house.

"I'm right here making breakfast, what are you yelling for?" she said.

As I walked into her kitchen, Demetri was walking out with an apple in his hand and a smile on his face.

"Ryan, you were supposed to just get the dick and beat your feet, not shack up with the nigga," I told her. I sat my bag on the back of my chair before pulling it out and sitting down.

"We are not shacking up. I enjoy his company," she smiled.

"Yeah, whatever. When I put a bullet in his rude ass, I'll make sure to find you someone else whose company is ten times better. That nigga got you dicked whipped, but its okay."

"Harlem, shut the hell up. No one is dick whipped. I know things with Enzo and I are fresh, but I see no sense in crying over spilled milk."

"Well alright then. I hear that. Now pass me a plate and tell me what you called me over here for."

Ryan made me a plate of eggs, turkey bacon, and french toast. She sat the plate in front of me before going to the fridge to get me a bottled water. She sat across from me with the serious look on her face.

"Ight, so yesterday, Alani calls me and tells me that Enzo is the reason she is in jail."

"Come again?" I asked. I was going to need her to repeat that shit one more time. Enzo was cold, but the nigga wasn't that bad.

"From the look on your face, I can tell that you heard what I said, but I'll repeat it because your ass is kind of slow. Enzo is a snitch bitch."

"Get the fuck out of here," was all I could say. Damn, I would have never guessed Enzo was a snitch, especially because of how close he and Isiah were.

"I couldn't believe it either, but you know what we have to do, right?"

"I already know. That's why Alani don't want Isiah and Ques coming to the bail hearing." I was saying the part about Isiah and Ques more so to myself. I couldn't believe this shit.

"Exactly, but I been thinking about that and I feel it would be best if we don't go to any of her hearings or the trial. We need to keep our distance from Alani so Enzo won't think anything is up. The longer we can keep him around us, the easier it will be to handle him when the time is right."

"Yeah, I agree. Isiah was blacking this morning about Alani not wanting him there. If none of us go, I think he will be able to handle the shit easier."

"Alani don't want the guys to know about Enzo tho." When she said that, I dropped my fork. I didn't see any good coming out of keeping this secret. Keeping this secret could possibly mess up my relationship with Isiah.

"Look, I don't know if I can do that. Don't you think Isiah should know that his right hand man is fucking shady?"

"If it was up to me, I would be down to tell the guys, but Alani doesn't want them to know. She thinks it will be for their benefit."

"This is some straight bullshit. How did things get so out of control?" the tears started flooding from my eyes. I was supposed to be the strong one in this situation, but for some reason, strength was the furthest thing from me.

"Harlem, don't cry. Now is not the time to show signs of weakness. If we want Alani out of jail, then we have to do what we have to do. Alani is counting on us, and so is the rest of the family. This is all on us and we have to rise to the occasion because there is no failing."

"You right," I told her and went back to eating.

"I'm gonna give you a minute to get yourself together," she got up and left out of the kitchen, giving me time to put everything in perspective.

It was crazy because on my way over here, I was thinking about how it was family over everything. Now it was time to put my money where my mouth was, and my ass started crying. I can't lie, I had a moment of weakness because what Ryan told me was totally unexpected. Never in a million years would I have thought I would be hearing how Enzo was a snitch. What was even more shocking was how Ryan seemed calmed about the whole situation. If anyone should have been crying, it should have been her. I guess Demetri was taking her mind off of things, which was a good thing. Ryan was too good of a person to have to deal with the bullshit alone. As far as Enzo was concerned, that nigga just awakened the beast in me. Lady Killers was about to be etched in his skin forever. Like I said before, it was family over anything, and I would lay my life on the line if it meant my family would be straight.

Chapter Four: Ques

"Ight, you good. You can go in now," the C.O. said to me.

I got up and walked into the visiting room, taking a seat all the way in the back to the far right. It was the day after Alani's bail hearing, and she insisted that I come see her. On the real, I didn't have nothing to say to her ass. Even in jail, her ass was still playing games like this shit was chess.

The Sunday before her bail hearing I get a call from her lawyer, Berkovich, saying how Alani didn't want me at the bail hearing, or any of her court dates. When that nigga told me that bullshit, I just hung up the phone and called Isiah to find out what the deal was. Come to find out, Berkovich had the same conversation with Isiah. Isiah said Alani didn't even want him to visit her. Isiah was pissed and in my eyes, he had every right to be. Alani was on some straight bullshit and all we were trying to do was help her get out of this fucked up situation.

She called me Monday night telling me how her bail was denied. Other than the details of her bail hearing, she wasn't saying too much of anything. When I asked her about not wanting Isiah to visit her, she tried to tell me some bullshit. She said it wasn't just Isiah she blocked from visiting, but it was the girls too. Chinky had the nerve to say it was because she got herself into this mess, so she was going to get herself out. If you let her tell it, she didn't want any of us stressing over her situation, which to me was straight bullshit. I told her I would be making a trip the next day to come see her, and she said it was a good idea.

"Ques," Alani smiled, taking me away from my thoughts. I looked at her as she sat across from me at the table. She didn't seem stressed or anything. I have seen jail break down the toughest niggas, but Alani seemed to be handling it well.

"Wassup?" I asked her with an eyebrow raised. I couldn't put my finger on it, but something was off about her. From the outside looking in, she seemed normal, but I knew Alani better than that.

"Nothing much. You know, taking it day by day," she shrugged.

"You need to put your brother and the girls on your visitor's lists. You're in jail, why would you want to cut off all communication from them?"

"Look, I don't know how else you want me to explain this. What I'm going through right now is something that I need to go through alone. I got myself into this mess and I'm going to get myself out. I don't want y'all coming up here with y'all sad ass facial expressions and shit. I'm good knowing that y'all are on the outside living it up the way y'all are supposed to."

"That's some bullshit and you know it Alani. I know you so you're gonna have to come better than that," I told her. If she thought that weak excuse was going to work on me, then she had another coming.

"I can't come better because what I said is how it is."

"Yeah ight, Alani."

"I didn't want you to come here so we could argue," she said.

"Then the fuck you let me come up here for? It seems like you don't want no one by your side during this time."

"Don't take this shit personal because it's not even that deep. You're making it a bigger deal than what it really is."

"Nah, don't even try that with me. I'm not making nothing bigger than what it is. I'm going off of what it seems like."

"I'm just going to come out and say what I have to say because I can't do this back and forth shit."

"Let's hear it," I smirked. There was nothing else that Alani could say that would piss me off more than I already was. She was doing the most right now and she couldn't even see it.

"I think we need to end things. We don't know how much time I'm looking at and I don't feel like you should waste your time on me, especially because we have only known each other for two months."

"That's what you want?" I asked to make sure because once I left, I wasn't coming back.

"Yeah. I want you to know this wasn't an easy thing for me to decide. I just feel like it has to be done. Everything I felt for you is real, and I still have those feelings. Now just isn't the right time to explore them," she said.

"Keep your fucking feelings because you not shit but a selfish fucking bitch. Did you even think how the fuck this would make me feel? A nigga is willing to do a bid for you and you want to end things. I was willing, able and ready to ride for your ass, but you can't even see that shit because all you care about is your fucking self. I didn't ever have to beg a bitch to be with me, and I'm not going to start now. I'll keep money on your books because that's what any real nigga would do for the chick he loves."

After saying my peace, I got up and left, leaving Alani there to deal with the words I just said to her. I got in my car, pulling out my phone and calling the only person I knew that could help me take my mind off of Alani.

"Ques, I'm sorry about the shit that happened at the club. I didn't expect things to go that far," Silver said as soon as she picked up the phone.

"Don't even trip about that. I need some pussy, where you at?"

"I'm home, but I don't think that is a good idea. I don't need no more drama coming from Alani and her little mutts." I laughed because Silver was trying to cop a plea, all the while throwing jabs.

"Fuck Alani. You scared of her or something?"

"No, I'm not scared of her. I just don't want to deal with anymore drama."

"Trust me, there won't be no drama. I'll be at your spot in an hour or two. Make sure you have a hot meal waiting for me."

I hung up the phone, not giving Silver a chance to respond. I pulled off away from the jail with no regrets about what I was about to do. Alani wanted to end things and I wasn't going to beg her to be with me. Fuck her was the only thought running through my mind at the moment. Shit, 2pac said it best, revenge is the sweetest joy next to getting pussy. It just so happened I was about to kill two birds with one stone.

* * * *

"Why you look so nervous? I'm not going to hurt you," I told Silver. I have been at her house for about thirty minutes.

Since I stepped foot in the door, she made sure to keep her distance from me. She was moving around and behaving like I had the plague or something. I didn't know what she was scared of because if I wanted to kill her, it would have happened when I first got here.

"I don't think you're going to hurt me, it's just that I've been through a lot these past few months, you know." She sat across from me as I continued to eat my shrimp Alfredo.

"Yeah, but everything you been going through is shit you brought on yourself, baby girl."

"You're right, and I want to leave the past in the past. On some real shit, I know I might come off as a thot or whatever, but that's not even me. I want the whole relationship, kids, and a family thing. I just don't know how to go about getting it."

"Fucking niggas on the first night isn't the way to go about it," I smirked.

"I guess, but I said all of that to say I'm not just trying to be a fuck to you. If you want pussy, I can give it to you this one time, but after that, there will be nothing else coming from me. I'm really thinking about going celibate until I get married."

"You're thinking about doing what?" I damn near spit out my water when I heard her say that shit.

"I'm thinking about going celibate. Damn, is it that much of a surprise?"

"Nah, it just caught me off guard. I think you wanting to change your lifestyle is a good thing. I just need you to bless this mic one last time."

"Anything for you," she purred.

I positioned myself in the chair so she could kneel in front of me. She pulled off my sweats and boxers, while locking eyes with me. I made sure to get my gun out the small of my back so it wouldn't hit the floor. Her tongue glided over her lips, making me anxious to feel it on my tip. She lowered her head, ready to put the tip in her mouth, when I cocked my pistol back and sent one straight to her head. I made sure to screw my silencer on before I left out the car.

Silver's body slumped to the floor as I turned around and kept on eating like nothing happened. I had every intention on coming over here, getting some pussy and then getting my revenge, but I couldn't do it. The feelings I still had for Alani wouldn't allow me to take it there with Silver. When I was done eating, I made me a to go plate because Silver cooked the shit out of that pasta. I then wiped down everything I touched and was out the door like I was never there.

Thoughts of Alani filled my head as I drove back home. I was feeling fucked up inside, but there was nothing I could do. I wasn't the type to keep a chick who didn't want to be kept. I may not have gotten pussy tonight, but at least I was able to get revenge for my baby. Even if Alani and I weren't together, she would always be my baby.

Chapter Five: Isiah

A nigga was out in these streets, hustling hard because I didn't know what else to do. Weeks turned into months and I still haven't heard anything from Alani. She dead ass cut off all communication with the outside. You knew she was serious about doing this bid on her own because she wasn't even talking to the girls. The only reason I knew what was going on with her trial is because her lawyer would call me with info from time to time. The info he was giving me wasn't even nothing big. He was feeding me with a long handle spoon, as if I was the one that got Alani locked. The whole situation was fucking me up on the inside, so I put all my effort into making money. I was neglecting Harlem like a muthafucker, but I just couldn't focus on us and our relationship. Thoughts of Alani and how she was doing consumed my thoughts on a 24/7 basis. It was fucked up, but I don't even think she cared.

Since Alani cut everyone else off, Harlem has been on some sneak shit. She doesn't bother me and I don't bother her. We still ate together and slept in the same bed, but that was as far as it goes. Sex was nonexistent in our relationship for the past month. There is no connection anymore. Circumstances just kind of got in the way of everything. As long as she wasn't fucking no other nigga, I was straight. I don't care how much I was neglecting her, she better take her neglected ass somewhere with Ryan. Her ass getting another dude was out of the question. Things were rocky right now, but once I got Alani out of jail, then we would be back straight. I just needed time.

"We been sitting here for over ten minutes and no one has said anything yet. We missing money by sitting in here," Kash complained.

"Nigga, chill the fuck out! If we asked you here, then it's for a reason," Ques said.

"Ques, you know I got nothing but respect for you and the big homie Isiah, but who's going to give me the money I'm missing out on. A nigga not balling like the three of you," he said, pointing to Enzo, Ques, and I. "I got about six mouths I need to feed."

I started laughing, even though what he said wasn't the least bit funny. I pulled my gun from my waist band and sat it on the table. Without saying anything, Ryan and Harlem pulled out their glocks, holding in each hand. I stood up from my chair, still laughing. I kicked it over, then slammed my fist on the table.

"Y'all muthafuckers will sit here for as long as I say. I'm the head honcho in this muthafucker. Y'all move to the beat of my fucking drum. Now if any of y'all got a fucking problem with the way I'm conducting business, then you can excuse yourself from the table. Best believe you won't be walking out of this bitch alive." I looked at every nigga sitting in this room. I looked deep into their eyes, looking for any trace of intimidation or nervousness in their eyes.

Having a team that was intimidated wasn't something I wanted. Having a team of niggas that are scared of you is equivalent to having a team of wolves in sheep clothing. They would act like they down for you until they saw an opportunity to take you out. Fear isn't something I wanted out of these niggas, I wanted respect.

"You the boss and all, but I'm not up for this fucking disrespect. I respect you and I expect the same in return. I'm not making no threats or nothing, but you're not the only nigga with a gun," Kash spoke. His tone wasn't loud, it was even and calm.

I nodded my head because I respected what he had to say. This little nigga had heart, unlike the rest of these muthafuckers in the room.

"You know what Kash, I commend you for the way you stuck up for yourself. You weren't disrespectful with the shit, but what you said was felt. For the rest of you muthafuckers, I need all of you to be on your job like your fucking life depends on it. I need you out here hustling like you may not wake up. I need y'all making this money like you only got twenty fours. If I'm out here grinding, y'all need to be grinding ten times fucking harder. As y'all already know, my sister got locked up a month ago. As far as her charges, I'm not too sure what they are right now," I lied. I didn't want to give these niggas too much, because for all I know, one of these niggas could be the reason she's in there.

"With her in jail, all eyes are on us. They think I'm going to drop the ball because my sister is jammed up. We not dropping shit over here though. The streets are fucking watching, so let's give them a fucking show. Now get the fuck out," I said smoothly, sitting back in my chair.

I watched everyone file out the room. Ryan and Harlem were now sitting at the table because it was now time for us to have a meeting of our own. I needed to come up with a way to get my fucking sister out of jail.

"Man, you be giving them little niggas too much leeway. You keep fucking around and they gonna rally up on your ass," Enzo said.

"Nigga, the fuck I tell you about questioning me and shit. I do what the fuck I want. You talking all that shit about what these niggas are saying, but where the fuck have you been? You been taking a lot of out of town visits." Enzo hasn't really been around since Alani got locked up. I thought the shit was strange as fuck.

"I know you not trying to say I have something to do with Alani sitting in fucking jail. Lani is like a sister me my nigga. You know how I roll; it's death before dishonor my nigga." I nodded my head at what he said, but I wasn't so sure if I believed him.

"Look, Lani is sitting in jail on a fucking murder charge. We need to do something to find out something," I sighed. The whole situation was stressing me the fuck out.

"I already told you what she told me a month ago. She wants to ride that bid out on her own," Ques shrugged. He was hiding his emotions well, but I knew him well enough to know it was fucking with him as much as it was fucking with me.

"That shit she said is straight bullshit. I don't know what the fuck is going on with Alani, but something isn't right."

"I can try to talk to her lawyer to see if she will talk to me or Ryan," Harlem offered.

"You do that shit. We paying that nigga, but he don't want to say shit," I stressed.

"At the moment, there isn't anything that we can do. We just need to keep our ear to the street and continue getting this money," Enzo said.

"I hear you nigga."

I got up and left because nothing was helping the situation. I need someone to tell me what the hell I needed to do in this situation.

"Isiah hold up," I heard Harlem yell after me.

I stopped at the entrance of the warehouse where our meeting was being held. I leaned up against the door, watching Harlem jog towards me. She was fucking beautiful. Nah, scratch that, she was breathtaking. Harlem deserved a lot more than what I was giving her right now.

"Isiah, you don't have to deal with this alone. We are all going through the same thing. The only way we are going to get over this is if we stick together," she said, looking at me.

"You right ma," I said.

"Ight, now let's go home so we can spend some time together." She smiled, leaning forward, kissing me.

I returned the kiss, slipping my tongue into her mouth. Kissing turned into touching, and touching turned into groping.

"I miss you," she purred, nibbling on my ear.

"I missed you more," I told her.

"Don't nobody wanna see that shit. Get a fucking room or something," Ques spat, coming into the hallway."

"Stop hating my nigga," I laughed. This was the first real genuine laugh I had in the last month.

"Don't be mad, Ques. Daddy, I'll be waiting for you in the car. Don't keep me and Ms. Kitty waiting too long," Harlem licked her lips in the most seductive way possible before walking away.

"Hating ain't in my blood. That's for your boy back there," he said.

"Where he at?"

"Back there talking to Ryan."

"Word?" I asked.

"Yeah, she wanted to talk to him. I don't know why she even wanna be in the same room as that nigga. I don't care what anyone say; that nigga ain't as true blue as you think he is. The only people who knew about Khalil getting killed was the crew. The niggas we got working for us might've suspected the shit because the nigga had beef with us, but other than that, they didn't have any real evidence about that shit."

"You might be on to something. Ight, this is what I want you to do. Get that young nigga Kash to follow this nigga. Tell him I'll pay him double what he makes in the trap. I need him to report back on everything. If Enzo is up to some shady shit, then we need to find out. As much as I don't want your suspicions to be true, if he is on some fuck shit, then it's lights out for that man."

"It ain't nothing to pull a trigger. I'll get on it asap though." Ques and I dapped each other up before walking out the warehouse and going our separate ways.

I got in the car feeling some type of way about Enzo's actions. He was definitely up to something. I just hope it didn't have anything to do with my sister. Enzo, Alani and I grew up together. The nigga was dead ass my brother; blood couldn't have made us any closer. If the nigga went against the family, then I would have no choice but to end his life. Oh, but trust, it wasn't going to be quick and easy. If Kash came back telling me Enzo had something to do with Alani being in jail, he was going to suffer for every day that Alani had to sit in jail. That was word to my moms.

Chapter Six: Enzo

"You didn't want to talk to me alone so you could kill me, right?" I chuckled lightly, but I was dead ass serious. I didn't expect to be having any conversations with Ryan after that bullshit happened with Ciara at her house.

"Enzo, if I was going to kill you, I wouldn't need to get you alone. I wanted to talk to you because I feel like we should talk about the whole Ciara situation. I may have overacted a little."

"You had every right to act the way you did. I'm the one that needs to apologize. I said a lot of things that were out of bounds. I definitely shouldn't have asked you to be my child's god mother. Well, my supposed to be child," I said, shaking my head. I honestly couldn't believe Ciara was pregnant by another nigga. That shit was karma for real.

"You know how the saying goes, what goes around comes around. All of that is in the past and I just want to move forward. I'm not saying that we are going to be best friends or anything, but I'm no longer going to hold hate in my heart for you. I decided to just let everything go and move on with my life."

"Who the fuck you moving on with? Ciara's brother?" Just the mention of her moving on had me hot. I couldn't see Ryan dating no one else but me. I was the first one to hit that pussy, which means I marked it just like how a dog marks his territory when he pees on a tree.

"Who said anything about moving on with a guy? You know what, that doesn't even matter. All I'm really trying to say is everything is good between us," she smiled.

I pulled her by the sweat shirt she had on, bringing her into an embrace. I couldn't help myself. The love I had for Ryan was still very apparent. I knew if I still loved her, she had to still love me. There was no way a love like ours could have died so fast and so easy.

"Enzo, what are you doing?" her voice trembled as I cupped her chin.

"Shhhhh," my lips were inches away from hers. The only reason I didn't go the whole way was because I wanted to see if she was going to fill the gap.

"We can't do this," she said, trying to fight the urge.

I already had her pants unbuttoned. I dipped my hand in her panties, gently tapping against her pussy.

"Why not, who's going to stop us? You want this just as much as I do. Don't fight it, just kiss me ma. Kiss me, Ryan," I taunted her.

We were literally sharing breaths as I waited to see what she was going to do. Ryan was hesitating on making the move, so I did it for her. I took my left hand out her panties wrapped it around her waist, roughly kissing her. It took her a minute, but she finally gave in to the kiss. She kissed me back hungrily. Kissing and groping, groping and kissing, everything became intense. Ryan pushed me away from her, stepped out of her jeans and panties, then lifted her sweat shirt over her head. She got on the edge of the desk and lifted her legs wide open. Her pussy was staring at me, begging me to come take it.

I unbuckled my jeans, stepping out of them and releasing the beast. I stroked my dick as Ryan fingered herself. The sight in front of me was one that was going to remain etched in my brain forever.

"Come give me what I want," she ordered.

I walked the short distance to the table, threw her legs over my shoulders and plunged into her without any mercy.

"Ohhhhhh," Ryan hissed.

I found my rhythm at the same time Ryan found hers. Her hips were bucking while I went deep sea diving. Ryan was wet as fuck. Her pussy was making that gushy sound. You know that sound mac and cheese makes when it's loaded with cheese.

"Fuck, you got some good pussy. I don't know why I ever let you get away," I grunted. I was trying my hardest not to bust so soon, but Ryan's pussy was doing something to me.

"Shut up and just give me the dick, Enzo. Fuck me better than the way you were fucking that young bitch," she moaned.

I picked up the pace, giving her all of me. She rubbed and tugged on her nipple, screaming out in pleasure.

"Let that shit go, Ryan. Don't hold back on a nigga. Fill the room with your sweet scent," I command.

I was giving her the best sex that I could muster up. I was praying that the sex was so good she got addicted to the dick and couldn't leave me alone. I know I did Ryan wrong, but I was ready to make up for it. With the way things were going in my life, I was going to need at least one person on my team. If a nigga was going to go to war, the only person I would want standing next to me is Ryan.

"Ahhhhh, I'm cumming," she squealed, tightening up. Her pussy walls were suffocating my dick.

"Fuck!" I spat, pulling out and releasing my nut on Ryan's stomach. I had every intention of cummin' inside of her, but at the last minute, I figured it wouldn't be the right time. I wasn't sweating it because I was going to have another opportunity to hit that pussy again, and when I did, was going to knock her ass up.

"Mhmmm, that was good," Ryan cooed, pushing me away from her and hopping off the table. I stopped her from going anywhere, and used my shirt to wipe off the cum from her stomach.

"It was, right" I agreed.

"Unfortunately, I have to go," she said.

"Damn, you just going to sex and leave a nigga. The least you could do is leave a couple of bills," I laughed, joking.

Ryan dug in her purse, pulling out her wallet. I looked on in amazement as she slipped three hundred dollar bills into my hand.

Leaning over, she whispered in my ear, "You're worth more, but that's all the money I have on me at the moment."

I smiled as she kissed me on the cheek, then strutted out the room like she was a model on the runway. Man, Ryan was that bitch, but most importantly, she was my bitch. She was a born killer and that's what I loved most about her. She didn't mind getting her hands dirty or riding shot gun. I wouldn't even compare her to Bonnie because she was above her. Ryan was in a league of her own, which was why I wanted and needed for her to be back on my team.

It's true what they say about men not realizing what they had until it's gone. I was the one to break things off with Ryan, but I missed her ass. I thought shit was greener on the other side, but was sadly mistaken. Ciara wasn't half the woman she portrayed herself to be when we were sneaking around. She didn't clean, and she could barely cook. The only thing she knew how to cook was the basic shit, like chicken and spaghetti. A nigga like me liked curry chicken and oxtails. Then her ass was needy as hell. I made my bed, so I decided to lay in it and act like everything was sweet between Ciara and I. After a while, I just couldn't take the shit anymore. The best thing for that child would be for us to co-parent.

I went back to get my baby and found her having a wet dream about another fucking nigga. I couldn't believe that shit. Then to make matters worse, Ciara's ass pops up talking about how the baby not mine and trying to spill all of a nigga's secrets. I would have never thought Ciara would betray me like that, but I have no one to blame but myself. I shouldn't have been pillow talking in the first place. But shit, good pussy has a way of making you do things you never wanted to do.

Now here I am trying to figure out a way I can get my baby back. I needed Ryan now, more than ever. Shit was about to hit the fan soon and I need her on my team. Alani cutting everything off wasn't something I expected, but I was happy as fuck that it happened. When her ass got arrested, I was ready to skip town with the money I had stashed. But since she wasn't talking to anyone, and her lawyer wasn't saying too much of anything, I had a little bit more time to get Ryan to see that with me is where she is supposed to be.

I know y'all thinking I'm some fuck ass snitch nigga, but do I give a fuck? Hell no. Y'all can't judge me because none of y'all know my side of things. Growing up, I was always in the shadow of Isiah. All I ever heard was Isiah and Enzo or Isiah this and Isiah that. Not once have I ever heard, Enzo and Isiah or Enzo out there making moves. Yeah, niggas in the hood knew me, but they didn't respect me, they tolerated me. Isiah had all the respect, which made no fucking sense to me. Everything we have, we built together. He never did more work than me, and I never did more work than him. Everything was straight fifty fifty between us.

The average person would say I was jealous of Isiah, which wasn't the case. Unless you were in someone else's shadow, you wouldn't know how I feel. As a man, I have to make a path for myself and create a legacy that niggas will be talking about twenty years from now. What better way to build that legacy than to take the nigga who overshadows me for everything he got. I didn't have a problem with Alani, she was just a causality in the war that was soon to come. Her ass could chalk it up to the game from the way I see things.

Chapter Seven: Ryan

I sped home trying to wash the stank off me from the dirty deed I just did with Enzo. Things weren't supposed to go that far. All I was trying to do was talk to him to let him know that we were on good terms. One thing lead to another and we ended up having sex. The sex wasn't even that fucking good. The shit was whack. I got more pleasure playing with myself, than I did from Enzo. When Enzo and I were together, I used to love his sex. The change could have been because Demetri has been slinging that dope dick my way. For the last month, Demetri and I explored every inch of each other's body, all the while getting to know each other. We did more than have sex, but the sex was amazing as hell.

"Fuck!" I yelled out loud. It just dawned on me that I cheated on Demetri.

The right thing to do was tell him, but I wasn't going to do that. If I told him, I would also have to tell him the plan Harlem and I had to get Alani out of jail. There was no way I was going to tell him when Ques and Isiah didn't even know. I was just going to take this shit to my grave and hope that my conscience doesn't try to kick in.

Harlem and I didn't have much time to come up with an elaborate plan on how to get rid of Enzo. The longer we prolonged the situation, the longer Alani would have to remain in jail. Alani was already in jail for a little too long, so we decided to use the one thing men couldn't deny. Pussy. My job was to get back close with Enzo, and right before the dirty deed happened, I would end his life.

I was a strong believer in the saying, no face no case. Enzo's body was going to be chopped to pieces and thrown into a meat grinder. There wasn't gonna be any jail time behind his snitch ass for anyone.

Enzo and I having sex pushed my timeline up a little because it showed he was willing and ready to fix things between us. His hope in reconciliation was also going to be his demise. I still couldn't fathom him being a snitch. The Enzo from back in the day lived and breathed the saying, death before dishonor. Somehow, he lost his way and turned into a person I didn't even know anymore.

Getting out the car, I decided to leave all my thoughts of Enzo at the door. There was no point in asking questions I didn't care to know the answer to. He was going to die, and that was the end of that. I walked into my house, ready to shower and just relax for the rest of the night.

Some people want it all but I don't want nothing at all. If it ain't you baby. If I ain't got you baby. Some people want diamond rings, some just want everything but everything means nothing if I ain't got you. Some people search for a fountain that promises forever young. Some people need three dozen roses and that's the only way to prove you love them.

Alicia Keyz's song "If I Ain't Got You" started blaring from my phone. I set the song for Demetri, which was corny, but it was kind of how I felt. I grabbed my phone out my back pocket, answering it before it went to voicemail.

"Hey, wassup?" I smiled, even though he couldn't see me.

"Nothing, just wanted to see how your day was ma?"

"My day was boring. I had a meeting with Isiah, but other than that it was uneventful."

"Since your day was uneventful, let me put some excitement in it."

"And how do you plan on doing that?" I acted like I was uninterested, but on the inside, I was happy as hell. I couldn't really explain how Demetri made me feel, but it was a feeling I never experienced before. Some might say I was moving too fast, but I didn't think so. I was simply going with the flow and living life.

"Unlock the door and let me in," I jumped off the bed and ran to the door, opening it and jumping into his arms.

"Let me find out you're missing the kid," he said, carrying me in the house and kicking the door closed.

"Always miss you when you're gone," I said without realizing it.

"Word?" he asked.

"I mean, not all the time," I tried to explain what I meant, but Demetri cut me off.

"If you miss me whenever I'm not with you, then that's how you feel ma. No need to hide that shit. I already know you're perfect for me, I'm just waiting for you to realize the same thing."

"Oh shut up," I punched him in the arm and buried my face in the crook of his neck. Whenever Demetri would say stuff like that to me, my face would always get flustered.

"My word is my bond ma," his hands cupped my ass as he brought me upstairs to my room.

He sat on my bed with me still in his arms. Nothing was being said between the two of us, we were just savoring the moment. This wasn't the first time we did something like this. On more than one occasion we would be wrapped in each other's arms, not saying anything. For some reason, no words needed to be said between us whenever we got like this. Our heartbeats did all the talking that we needed them to.

"Oh no, we can't do that," I said, hopping off his lap. His hands were going towards my sweet spot, and I couldn't have that. I got side tracked from showering when Demetri called. There was no way I was going to fuck Demetri right after I fucked Enzo.

"Why not, you bleeding?"

"No, I just don't want our relationship to be built on sex," I lied.

"You already know I hate fucking liars, so I suggest you try that again."

"Try what again?" I questioned.

"You on some bullshit, Ryan. What happened?" The look he was giving me was breaking my heart.

"I'm not on anything. I been talking with Harlem and she thinks I'm moving too fast. I just want to slow things up a bit." The lies were rolling off my tongue as if they were the actually truth.

"So now we care about what other people say? Other people's opinions are going to determine what goes on in this relationship? Is that what the fuck you're telling me?" Demetri wasn't yelling, but I could definitely hear the bass in his voice.

"No, it's not that, it's just…" the lies that were once rolling off my tongue so smoothly, were now stuck in my voice.

"Exactly," he pushed me off of him and went to walk towards my bedroom door.

I jumped up and rushed to the door, closing it and leaning my back up against it. There was no way I was going to let his ass leave over this bullshit.

"I don't hit women Ryan, but with the way that I'm feeling, you're liable to end up knocked the fuck out."

"You really going this hard all because I don't want to give you sex? Is sex the only thing that you wanted?" I sassed.

"Ryan, do you hear how fucking stupid you sound? You really going to try and say that I'm going hard for sex like you're not standing here lying in my face. I'm not that dude who cheated on you. I can handle the truth, and I can definitely handle you, but what I can't handle is a bitch that lies to my face."

By the time he finished the word face, my hand had connected with his face. I was way out of bounds, but he called me a bitch. I started this shit, but I didn't expect him to disrespect me like that.

"You putting your hands on me isn't something I wanted to bring out of you. This shit right here," he said waving his finger between both of us, "isn't even us. Now if you want to tell me the truth, then I'm all ears. Or you can keep those lies you're telling me and move the fuck out my way, and I'm gone for good.

I quickly thought about the choice I needed to make. About seventy-five percent of me wanted to lie just so I wouldn't have to admit to sleeping with Enzo. But the twenty-five percent wasn't going to let me continue lying to the man I saw my future with.

"I slept with Enzo," I whispered.

"That's all you had to say from the jump. Now move."

I stepped to the side, allowing him to leave out. I stood in my bedroom doorway, waiting to hear the front door open and slam close. The sound I was looking for never came. I walked from the back of my house into the living room. Demetri was sitting on the couch, watching TV.

"You're not going to leave?" I asked.

"Nah," was all he said.

"I'm so sorry, Demetri. I swear I didn't mean for that to happen," I said trying to plead my case without giving too much away.

"I don't even want to hear that shit. When we made things official between us, that meant we didn't keep secrets from each other. That shit also meant we didn't lie to each other. I'm not God, so I don't judge. You slipped up and fucked your ex, there is nothing I can do about the shit because the shit is already done. Am I going to let one fuck up run me out the door, hell nah, but that one fuck up is all the fuck you get. Just because I'm not in the streets doesn't mean I'm pussy. I get down with the best of them, and street niggas aren't the only ones with fucking guns.

I accepted you being around that nigga because y'all work together or some shit. What I'm not going to accept is you back sliding. I'm man enough to deal with your mistake, so you need to be woman enough to not do it again."

"Okay." Shit, there wasn't nothing left to be said besides okay.

"Go wash that nigga the fuck off you. I'm chilling down here tonight. You on your own."

I really wanted him to cuddle with me tonight, but I wasn't going to push my luck. I would accept sleeping alone because I was the one in the wrong. The thing that surprised me the most was that he didn't leave. Any other nigga would have hemmed me up and chocked me out for sleeping with another dude, but Demetri didn't do any of that. I could tell he was mad about the situation, but he didn't let it take him out of character, and I could appreciate that. I needed to hurry up and handle Enzo so I could fully explore things with Demetri. If he played his cards right, he might be the lucky one to adorn my last name.

Chapter Eight: Harlem

Last night I fell in love with Isiah all over again. Since Alani has been in jail, there has been a strain on our relationship. Isiah and I haven't really clicked like we used to. We were both caught up in our own worlds, neglecting each other. But last night helped remind me of all the reasons I loved him. I wouldn't even say we had sex because it was so much more than that. The way our bodies intertwined as we brought each other to gut wrenching orgasms was cosmic. Our bodies fell in sync with one another as if they were meant to be one. If I didn't have this IUD in me, I would be pregnant. I'm kind of mad I have the IUD inside of me. The baby that would have been created would be a blessing for sure.

I quietly got out of bed and tip toed out of the room, trying my best not to wake Isiah. It was 7:50 in the morning and I was expecting a phone call from Alani at eight. Isiah and Ques thought she shut everyone out, but that wasn't the truth. I opened up a separate phone line where she could call me without Isiah knowing. Keeping this secret from Isiah was killing me, but it was something that needed to be done. Once everything was handled, I would tell him.

Ten minutes passed and my phone rang at eight on the dot.

"You have a collect call from Alani. Do you accept the charges?"

"Yes," I said into the phone.

"Girl, I need y'all to hurry up and send me some food or something," she said talking in code.

"You should have a package in a week. Ryan is handling everything. It's taking a little longer because Ryan wants to make sure she doesn't forget anything that you need."

"I know, but tell her I need my stuff like yesterday," she sighed. The frustration in her voice was evident. I felt bad that she had to go through this, but she wouldn't be in the situation for much longer.

"We got you, I promise," I told her.

"How are Ques and Isiah doing?"

"Ques is walking around acting like he isn't hurt behind this shit. Isiah on the other hand is hurting bad Lani. You should at least call him every once in a while."

"I can't do that. You know how Isiah can get. This is what's best for all of us. I promise you if I didn't think this was the best option then I wouldn't be doing it. I'm hurting just like he is. If not the same, then more. My brother is my world, and not being able to talk to him is killing me."

"I know Alani, I know," I sighed. We had this same conversation whenever we got on the phone. I always tried to get her to at least talk to Isiah on the phone, and she would always say no.

"Look, I have to go. Tell Ryan I love her."

"Okay."

"Harlem, I promise you no communication is the best. I love you girl."

"Love you too, Alani," I whispered, then hung up the phone.

I sat on the couch crying my eyes out because the whole thing was stressful as hell. All of us were running on emotion, which wasn't healthy. I couldn't wait for this whole thing to be over with. Once it was, I was going to suggest that everyone walk away from the life we lived. We didn't need to continue risking our freedom because we all had money. I couldn't take no one else being in jail. This shit was for the birds, and I was no longer with it.

"Harlem, are you crying?" I heard Isiah say, walking into the living room. He must've heard me sniffling because he couldn't see my face.

"No my nose is just a little stuffy." I quickly wiped my face trying to hide any evidence of tears.

"Yeah, but let me talk to you real quick. Things between us have been rocky, and it's my fault. The whole Alani thing is fucking with me."

"It's okay, don't even sweat it," I told him. I didn't want him feeling bad about the way he was treating me because I wasn't being fully honest with him.

"Nah, that shit isn't okay. I should never neglect the one I love because I got too much on my plate. Ima man, and as man, I should be able to handle everything with ease."

"Well alright, daddy," I giggled.

"I've been thinking about stepping out of the game too."

"Really, why?" I acted concerned on the outside, but on the inside I was happy as hell.

"The only reason I started hustling was so Alani and I would be straight. Both of us got more money than we actually need, so there is no reason to keep doing the shit. I rather invest my money in a couple of business and make that legit money than keep risking my life in this street shit."

"You already know I'm down for whatever you want to do."

"That's why I love your ass," he kissed me then got up and headed back towards the back.

The Enzo thing was supposed to be taken care of by the end of the week, but I wanted to get it over with now. I picked up my phone sent Ryan a text, letting her know I was on my way to her house. There was no point in dwelling on the situation. The faster we took care of the problem, the faster we could get back to how things were supposed to be.

Chapter Nine: Isiah

Harlem thought I was dumb, but I wasn't. Even though I was busy handling shit in the streets, I have noticed Harlem getting out of bed at a certain time for about fifteen minutes, then coming back. This morning when she got out of bed, I waited a couple of seconds before going to find where she went to. I found her ass on the couch, talking on the phone. I couldn't hear much that was being said, but I did hear her say that she loves Alani. That right there pissed me off because Alani was supposedly not talking to anyone. She started crying, and that's when I made my presence known. I comforted her, even though I was pissed off. I should've known better than to think Alani wouldn't talk to her girls. The three of them were keeping a secret, and I was going to get down to the bottom of it. My sister's freedom was on the line, and there were games being played.

Times gettin' hard but a nigga still getting' it. Young rich niggas in this motherfucker. When you wake up before you brush your teeth, you grab your strap nigga. Only time you get down on your knees shooting craps, nigga. Fuck what you heard, God blessin' all the trap niggas. Weighed 1008 grams on the spot. I got a lower case T across my chest. Your crack house doin' numbers then you blessed. You move your momma to a crib from the 'jects. It's so much alcohol and kush on my breath. We prayin' five times a day to catch a plug. A few beef pies stashed in the trunk. Shoot dice all day and sell dust. You loaded up, they talkin' shit, you gone bust. Told yourself a million times, you don't give a fuck. Sold over a million dimes, hangin' in the cut. Sold over a million dimes, I don't give a fuck.

I rapped along to Future's song "Trap Nigga" as it played from my phone. I let the song play out before picking up my phone to see who called. I saw it was Ques and went to hit him back, but before I could click his name, a text came through.

Ques: Come through, got some info.

If it was the info that I thought it was, then that was fast as hell. I put my phone on the charger, then jumped in the shower. After washing up a couple of times, I got out and threw on some clothes. Snatching up my keys and phone, I was ready to head out the door. I looked around the house for Harlem, but she wasn't there. I sent her a text letting her know I was going to be with Ques. I got in my car and drove off. I was anxious to find out what info he had for me. I had a feeling it had something to do with Enzo. Enzo and I have been like brothers for as long as I could remember. If he was on some snake shit, then I would be fucked up. I didn't let just anyone get close to me and my sister. So if Enzo did have something to do with Alani being in jail, there would be a whole bunch of repercussions.

* * * *

"Kash put me on to some shit last night after I told him to tail Enzo," Ques began to say, but I cut him off.

"Then why the fuck didn't you bring it to my attention last night?"

"Isiah, chill the fuck out because I'm not your fucking lap dog, ight? I didn't bring you the information because I told Kash to make sure he was one hundred about the shit. He hit me back at like four in the morning talking about Enzo is working for the Feds. Kash says he watched Enzo get into a black Lincoln town car. The car didn't pull off or nothing, they just sat in the car for about thirty minutes, then Enzo got out and went back to the crib."

"If he working with the Feds, then why would he go back to his crib? Shouldn't they have put him into some type of witness protection or something?"

"He probably didn't want to go because if he would've went, then we would have put two and two together. I still got Kash following him and shit."

"Ight, let me know if the little nigga finds out anything else," I told Ques.

"I'm about to send some of my geek niggas over there to bug his house. He working with the police, which means they recording every fucking thing. I doubt he wore a wire to the meeting, but you know sooner or later he's gonna call us to his house to discuss business. I'm not trying to be out here getting caught slipping."

"Ight," was the only thing I could think to say.

I dapped Ques up then left out his house. I got in my car and just sat there, trying to make sense of this whole thing. Why the fuck would Enzo be working with the Feds? It's not like he could have gotten jammed up because we don't touch the product. I didn't want to sound like a bitch, but this was really fucking with me. Enzo was my fucking brother and to find out he was going against the team, hurt like hell. I never pictured Enzo being a snitch, but sometimes it's the nigga that you think would have your back through it all that fucks you over.

He's probably the reason Alani was in jail. No one outside of our circle knew what the fuck happened to Khalil, and with the new information, all fingers pointed to him. It was okay though, because like the old saying goes, snitches get stitches.

Chapter Ten: Enzo

The pressure was on for me to get some type of information on Isiah. Last night I met up with Agent Mitchell to talk about everything that was going on. From what she said, Alani's trial would be starting early next week, so we needed to get Isiah now. We agreed to meet up at eight this morning to go over some strategies. After talking to her for nine hours, we finally came up with a plan. When I first started working with the Feds, they bugged my house. The plan was to get Isiah to come over and start talking about business. The only reason I didn't suggest this before was because Isiah never talked about business outside of his house or the warehouse. I always thought it was odd, but never questioned it. This was my last resort, so I was going to make it do what it do and get something. On the drive back to my crib, I called him and told him to meet me at my crib.

Right after I finished up with Isiah, I needed to get back to things with Ryan. What happened between the two of us yesterday was amazing, and I couldn't just sit around waiting for her to call. Nah, I needed to make my move, and that was exactly what I was going to do. Wine her, dine her and then whisk her ass away to a deserted island somewhere. As I pulled up to my house, I saw Isiah sitting in his car. I got out and hit him with the head nod, letting him know to follow me in the house. He was ending a phone call when he walked through the door.

"Wassup my nigga?" I greeted him.

"Ain't shit. You know how it be," he smirked, sitting on my couch.

"Money is the motive though, right?" I said, trying to get him to slip up.

"I'm just worried 'bout my sister right now. Money isn't always the motive. Happiness is."

"True that, but I want to talk to you about something."

"I would hope so since you called me over here," he laughed.

"I just want to apologize for overstepping my boundaries with some shit. The way you handle your business is exactly that. I shouldn't be putting in my two cents when they are not needed."

"No need to apologize. I already told you what it was and left that shit right where it was yesterday."

"Ight, I just wanted to make sure we were still cool. Seems like ever since Ques came back into the fold, we been drifting apart." I was trying my hardest to get him to say something incriminating, without incriminating my damn self.

"If niggas are drifting apart, it doesn't have to do with Ques. Ques is like a little brother to me, even before he got locked up. You know that. When he got out, we picked up right where we left off. The brotherhood you and I have has nothing to do with Ques because he wasn't around when we were growing up. If you feel a rift, maybe you need to ask yourself if you're the cause. Since Lani got locked up, you been real distant and taking trips and shit out the blue. Maybe I need to start questioning your motives and shit."

"Don't even try to play me like that. From the way shit is sounding, you trying to make seem like I'm not loyal. Shit, don't talk in riddles, come off top with what needs to be said." I was more so nervous than mad. Isiah finding out what I was into was a sure death sentence.

"Nigga, there is no need to come off top with what I'm trying to say because we both know what I'm talking about. You know just as well as I do that you been on some fuck shit lately. I don't know exactly what you got going on, and I don't need to know. When the time is right, you will tell me what I need to know. In the meantime, I'm going to distance myself from you."

"The fuck you mean distance yourself from me? We break bread together my nigga." My hands were sweating because this eerie feeling was looming over my head. Isiah had said in so many words that he knew what was going on, and he didn't want any parts of it.

"I can't break bread with a nigga I don't trust. Shit, I guess you can consider this me giving you your walking papers. Your services are no longer needed."

"The fuck you just say?" I yelled standing up. "We built this shit together and you're gonna try to give me my walking papers like I'm some chump." This is one of the reasons why I was doing what I was doing. Isiah always tried to act like he had the upper hand. His word wasn't engraved in stone. No nigga was going to tell me that I couldn't continue making money. This nigga wasn't my fucking daddy.

"The fuck you so mad for, jumping up and yelling and shit. Enzo, you know me, and you know I'm not about that rah rah shit. You also know that my word is my bond nigga. All this yelling and shit is making you look more like a bitch than you already do."

"Isiah, that's how we doing it now? You're throwing jabs and shit. I look like a bitch now?" I laughed, biting my bottom lip.

"Nigga you always looked like bitch. Now you have the attitude to match. You can't blame me for nothing that I'm saying right now. Your actions led me to the decision I made, and my decision is final."

"You might run these fucking little niggas in the street, but you don't run me."

"I never said I ran anyone. Those are your words, not mine. The only thing I do is make a way for me and my family."

The more he talked, the more pissed I became. It was as if he knew exactly what I was trying to do.

"Get the fuck out my house!" I yelled, sounding just like a scorned bitch.

"I didn't want to be here in the first place. The only reason I came is because I thought it would be the right thing to do to tell you the shit face to face. My family is dead to you and so am I. You on your own my nigga."

"On the real, I don't give a fuck about your family or anything else that has to do with you. I'm on a come up of my own. I'ma show all you pussy ass niggas who the fucking boss is. And when I get my come up, I'm going to make sure they give me your head on a fucking gold platter," I spat. My words were laced with venom. Everything that I said to Isiah was the truth. I didn't give a fuck about him and his family, which was why Alani was sitting in jail. If I had my way, she would be doing life.

"Is that a threat my nigga? You already know I don't take threats lightly. You can make all you want, but what you won't do is come for my family like we did something wrong. You're the one that went and fucked everything up. It's funny because you really think I wasn't going to find out. Nigga, New York City is mine and I carry Brooklyn on my back. Trust me, my city got me, but most importantly, I got my family," he smirked then got up and walked out the door like nothing happened.

This was his city for the time being. The nigga may not have said what I needed him to say about his dealing with drugs, but he did me one better. If I were to turn up missing or dead, all the Feds would have to do is listen to the recording from today. Isiah would then be in jail for my murder. Shit, I was gonna be winning from my grave, and that's something only a real boss could do.

Chapter Eleven: Ryan

"I'm surprised Demetri didn't choke your ass for that shit. You're my girl and all, but that shit is foul. You weren't supposed to fuck him, Ryan," Harlem said.

She has been at my house all day doing nothing but talking my ear off about how we need to get rid of Enzo tonight. I thought it was way too soon, but she said it was for the best. When I got up this morning, Demetri was gone and I haven't heard from him all day. I felt bad, but there was nothing else I could say but I was sorry. I wasn't ready to tell Demetri that I only slept with him so it would be easier to kill him. I didn't think Demetri was ready to know that aspect of my life.

"Ryan, are you listening to me?" Harlem questioned. In all honesty, I tuned her ass out a long time ago. I wasn't in the mood to hear her talk about my fuck ups. Demetri was already mad at me, so her going in on me was a waste of time.

"Harlem, I already know what I did was fucked up. I don't need you going in on me too. You were supposed to come over here to tell me this plan that you had to make it easy to get rid of Enzo."

"No need to catch a tude with me sissy. I was just saying if it was me, I wouldn't let that nigga stick his dick back in me."

"But you're not me, so let's move along please," I laughed.

"Anyway, I have this tube of stuff that you stick inside your vajayjay like a tampon. Since you already let him fuck, it shouldn't be too much to let him eat you either."

"How am I supposed to explain a tube in my pussy?"

"Just tell him that it's a surprise for him. Better yet, blind fold his ass then guide his mouth to your pussy, and pull the string. By the time he gets a taste of the poison, it will be a little too late."

"You really think that shit is going to work?" It sounded like a good plan, but sticking a tube of poison in my pussy didn't sound too appealing to me.

"I know it's going to work. Do you think I would let you go through with something I wasn't sure about? If I could do it myself, I would, but you know Enzo only has eyes for you. Don't think too much into it. Just be natural. If you need me, I'll be right outside with our young guns," she said.

"I swear to God, Harlem, none of that shit better soak into my pussy. If I can't have kids because of this shit, I'm going to kick your ass and you're naming your first born after me," I scolded her.

"Ryan, you are over exaggerating. Nothing is going to happen to your pussy. Would you feel better if I stuck it inside my pussy first," she asked, holding the vial of poison in her hand.

"Ewww no. I don't want that shit in your pussy, then I have to put it in mine. That's like sharing the same dick. We close, but we are not that close."

"Did you just come for me?" Harlem laughed. "You tripping. There isn't anything wrong with my pussy. This pussy clean and this pussy squeaky," she laughed, patting her pum pum as if it was on fire.

I laughed with her because she was stupid as hell, but that's what I loved most about my girl. She knew how to turn a serious moment into a funny one. We continued talking about the plan, when my house phone started ringing. That shit was odd as hell because no one ever called my house phone. I never even really gave the number to anyone.

"Who is that calling your house phone?" Harlem asked.

"I don't even know." I ran over to the window where I left my phone on the base and picked it up.

"Hello?"

"Good, you picked up. Ryan, I need you to come over to my house now. I have some things I need to get off my chest."

"Enzo?" I questioned. "You're talking too fast. I can't understand what you're saying."

"Look, just come over and I'll explain everything then. Please Ryan, I'm begging you. I need you more now than I ever did before. Just tell me you're coming over."

"I'll be there in twenty," I told him and hung up the phone.

"Why you look like that? What did Enzo say to you?" Harlem asked.

"He needs me to come over, but he didn't sound the same. Something about him seemed a little off." I sat on the couch while I was in a daze. Enzo's whole demeanor was off, and I didn't like it.

In the years that I have known him, I never heard worry in his voice until tonight's phone call.

"Well, that's great. Now you don't have to come up with an excuse as to why you need to see him," Harlem smiled.

"Harlem, did you hear anything I said besides the fact that he wants me to come over. Something is off about Enzo. He was talking a mile a minute and his words were being jumbled together."

"I'm sure it's nothing. There is no need for you to worry because I'll be right outside. I promise you I won't let anything happen to you, okay? This isn't anything that we haven't done before," she said, trying to calm me down, but it wasn't working.

"You're wrong. We haven't done anything like this before. I'm about to kill the man I once loved. Don't get me wrong, he deserves what he is about to get, but I still love him you know. If he really does need help and I just ignore that, what kind of person does that make me?" I didn't know where all this second guessing started coming from, but it was freaking me out.

"Ryan, you need to cut it out, ight. You are doing what needs to be done so your sister can be free. Everything Enzo is getting is stuff that he brought on himself. Don't question the type of person you are because of someone else's actions. Now hurry up and put the vial in your twat so we can go."

"I am not putting this in my twat right now. I'll do it before I get out the car. Just make sure you got our young niggas on standby. Call them after I go inside the house."

"Ight, boss lady. Let's do this."

I got up and changed my clothes. I put on a PINK sweat suit and a pair of Nikes so it looked like I dropped everything and rushed over to his house. I threw my hair in a half up half down do, and was out the door with Harlem. I was fine the entire car ride, but as soon as we pulled up in front of his house, my hands got sweaty and my throat got dry. For some reason, every time I thought about killing Enzo, I felt like I was doing something wrong. I have killed plenty of people, but Enzo seemed to be my most difficult task.

"Don't worry about anything, Ryan. Just use your sex appeal and everything will be fine, I promise. This is our last mission, and after this, we are out of the game for good. Alani will be home and our family will be whole again."

"I got this," I said more to myself than to Harlem.

I slipped my hands in my sweats, sticking the vial inside of me. When I felt comfortable enough, I exited out the car and knocked on his door. I only got in two good knocks before Enzo came to the door.

"You came," he smiled, pulling me into a hug. The embrace we shared was an uncomfortable one. My body cringed at his touch. I pulled away and walked inside with him.

"I'm so happy you came, Ryan. That means we still have a chance."

"Have a chance at what?" I asked as he closed the door.

"At being together. Now before you say anything, I already know that I fucked up big time by fucking with Ciara, and I'm truly sorry for that. I should have never stepped out on you. If I had a problem with our relationship, then I should have brought it to you so we could figure it out together. I want things to go back to how they were when we first got together. I want that old thing back ma." He walked towards me, caressing my arm and I pulled away.

"When we had that talk, it went further than what it should have. Sex wasn't supposed to happen."

"It might not have been what you planned, but it happened, so that must mean something."

"What is it supposed to mean Enzo?"

"That we are supposed to be together."

"How can we be together when I don't even trust you? You're not the same Enzo I once loved. You turned into a person I don't even recognize."

"I'm trying to get back right, but I need you by my side, Ryan. Nothing feels right unless you're there with me. I want to leave all the bullshit that has happened in New York and get away. Just you and I. We can start over somewhere fresh and somewhere new. We can even leave the states."

"Leave the states? Enzo, why would I leave the states when my friends are here? Not even my friends, *our* friends are here."

"I don't have no fucking friends!" he spat.

"That's right, they aren't our friends, they're our family. You just want to up and leave them behind?"

"The only family I got is you. Isiah ain't my family, and neither is that fuck boy Ques. None of them give a fuck about me, and I don't give a fuck about them. All I need in this life of sin is you. Well money and power too, but most importantly, you. Come with me, Ryan. We can have as many kids as you want and a big ass house that you can decorate. All I want to do is turn our house into a home," he whispered in my ear.

His teeth grazed my ear as his tongue slithered down my neck. I tried to stop my body from tensing up, but Enzo caught on.

"Relax ma. I'm not going to hurt you. Let me take care of you. Let me be one with your mind, body and soul. Let me in bae, just let me in," he moaned.

Enzo swept me off my feet and laid me against the floor. A million things were going on in my head as he pulled my sweats down. It was now the moment of truth, and a part of me wanted to push him away. I honestly didn't think I was strong enough to do it. I had to keep telling myself this wasn't about me. I was doing this for my family.

"Hold on," I told him. I stopped him just in time before he could get my panties off. "I want you to lick the cat blind folded," I purred.

"Oh word? You're into that kinky shit," he smirked.

I sat up a little so I could take my shirt off and I passed it to him. I watched him tie it around his head and bring his face back towards my pussy. I pulled my panties down while pulling the string at the same time. Putting my hands on the back of his head, I guided him towards my tunnel. His tongue touched my opening and my body froze.

"What the fuck!" he shouted. I scooted away from him and looked on as his tongue began to swell. I snatched the bottle out of me just as his mouth began to foam. Enzo somehow snatched the shirt off from around his eyes and looked at me with so much pity. I felt bad for him, but there was nothing I could do. His eyes were bulging out of his head and he was choking. The foam stopped dripping and he stopped moving all together. I snatched my sweats back up and grabbed my phone out of the pocket.

"Harlem, I don't know what you gave me to give this nigga, but you need to come in here. This nigga's tongue damn near exploded in his mouth," I panicked.

"Calm down. We are coming inside now," she said and hung up the phone.

I ran upstairs to his bedroom, found one of his old t-shirts and threw it on. When I came back downstairs, Harlem and two niggas I didn't know were in the house, looking at his body.

"How long did it take for him to go under?" she asked.

"I don't know, maybe like a minute," I told her.

"Carry his ass out and bring him out to the truck. Take him to that old ass meat place up in Queens. You know what to do with the body, and I don't want no fuck ups. Y'all fuck up, then you pay with your fucking life. You hear me?" Harlem asked them.

Both dudes nodded their head before picking up the body. I waited until they were gone to say something to Harlem.

"We are going to follow them, right?"

"Duh. You think I would really just let them go off on their own. Hurry up and help me wipe everything down. Once we're done, we are going to go to Queens. They shouldn't be that far ahead of us."

"Okay," I whispered.

"Don't beat yourself up about this shit. Alani will be home, and that's all that matters. Enzo wasn't shit but a snake anyway."

"I know. Let's just hurry up so we can get this shit over with," I told her.

I couldn't wait to get home. As soon as I walked in the door, I was going to call Demetri and tell him to bring his ass over. I wanted nothing more than to cuddle with him and forget about everything that has happened today. Enzo was now dead, and all the hurt and pain he had caused me went right along with him. I thought I was going to be fucked up behind killing him, but I honestly felt a sense of relief. I felt like a weight had been lifted off of my shoulder and now I could live my life and give my love to someone who deserved it.

Chapter Twelve: Alani

Two Weeks Later

Walking out of this crusty ass jail had me feeling like Cookie. I strutted my ass out of there like the world owed me something and I was coming collect. After the five weeks I spent in jail, I had a whole new outlook on life. The little things I took for granted before I got locked up, were now going to be the things I cherished the most. Not being able to come and go as I pleased was my biggest issue. I hated being told what to do, or even being on someone else's schedule. Being in jail could really mess with a person's mental state if they didn't handle everything correctly. Shit, I would rather die than go to jail. That shit really had a way of fucking with you.

"Oh shit, look who it is. Let me find out that jail house food was doing the body good," Harlem smiled as I walked towards them. Ryan and Harlem were the only people who knew that I was getting out. I wanted to go home and cook a family meal and surprise everyone else.

"Trust me, it wasn't the food that helped me get my body this way." I couldn't lie, my body grew out in the last few weeks. My hips spread, while it seemed like my stomach shrunk. In my spare time, I did work out a little. Working out wasn't something I wanted to do before, but it helped me keep a clear head. It was definitely one of the things I was going to take from jail and incorporate into my regular life.

"I'm just happy to see you," Ryan said, rushing over to me and hugging me.

I hugged her back then took a step back to get a good look at my girls. Harlem looked the same, but Ryan was glowing. She had that 'I get good dick on the regular' glow.

"Ryan, why you glowing and shit?"

"You picked up on that too," Harlem laughed. "I think she's pregnant, but I don't say much."

"Shut up, Harlem. No one is pregnant," Ryan whined.

"Uh huh. Well tell me all about the nigga that got you shining brighter than the sun." Harlem and Ryan sat in the front, while I got in the back of Harlem's car. Feeling the crisp winter air against my skin was amazing to me.

"No nigga got me glowing; I just finally feel good with myself. I'm truly at peace with myself, and the feeling is amazing," Ryan said.

"Girl, there is no reason for you to lie. Alani ain't nobody," Harlem chimed in.

"I'm not lying," Ryan laughed.

"Well if you're not going to tell her, then I will. Ryan has been getting dicked down proper by Demetri."

"Wait, Ciara's Demetri?" I questioned, shocked. I know they had a little chemistry, but I didn't know it turned into a relationship.

"The next day after you get locked up, Enzo's ass shows up at my house talking about he wants me back and shit. The whole thing was creepy because he caught me having a wet dream about Demetri. Any who, as I'm walking downstairs with Enzo right behind me, I hear one of my windows break. Ciara was at my house acting a god damn fool, spilling all the tea. Come to find out, the baby isn't even really Enzo's. While he was creeping with her, then coming home to me, her thot ass was creeping with the next nigga. She only said it was his because the other dude got locked.

When she was at my house, she told me how Enzo was pillow talking and how he's lucky she don't tell on his fraud ass, then she left. I got Enzo out of my house, called Harlem, and we took a ride to Ciara's mama's house. She told us Enzo was a snake and all this other bullshit. I didn't want to believe it because I didn't have proof. When Harlem and I were leaving, we ran into Demetri. One thing led to another and you know how that shit can go," Ryan shrugged.

"I owe that nigga a bullet for how he was talking to me on the phone," I laughed, but was dead ass serious. After we cooked dinner and everyone came over, I was going to make sure I got Tiffany. I missed my baby something terrible.

"Shut up. You're not going to shoot my baby. You need to work on getting your baby back," Ryan said.

"So what are you going to do about Ques? If you ask me, he is the nigga for you. He the only one that can put up with your slick mouth and hot tempered ways," Harlem added.

"I don't even know. Ques was hurt when I ended things with him. He probably feels like I keep playing with his heart and shit," I sighed.

"The good thing is, he hasn't been fucking with any new bitches," Harlem said.

"True," I told them, ending the conversation.

For the five weeks I was away, thoughts of Ques invaded my mind. I constantly questioned myself about if cutting him off was the right thing to do. I never second guessed myself with any decision I made, but that one was a constant battle. I missed him so much that I was willing to put all the killing shit to an end and become a house wife. I mean popping out kids and cooking breakfast, lunch and dinner. For Ques, I would become domesticated in a heartbeat.

For so long, I have been wishing and looking for that one dude that would want to go through it all with me. I mean through the good and the bad, the cute and the ugly. When I finally got that one person to hold it down, I became scared. The way Ques felt about me was so strong that it scared me. Now I was wishing I would've just been all the way honest with him. If he didn't want to fuck with me anymore, then I would just have to deal with it. I couldn't blame him or get mad because it was something that I put on myself. If he chose to walk away from me, then it was something I would just have to handle and be okay with.

* * * *

"Harlem, we could have had dinner at our own house," Isiah said as he walked in the door with Ques behind him.

"Isiah, shut the hell up. I figured we could have like a family kind of dinner over here. With everything that has been going on, I think we really need to sit down as a family. Our family values are slipping, and I don't like it. Now you will go into that kitchen, sit the hell down and enjoy the dinner that we have made for your ass." I told Isiah before turning my attention to Ques. "Hey Ques wassup."

I was peeking from the dining room, listening to Harlem give my brother the run down. It took everything in me not to run out into the living room and give them hugs. A couple of tears dropped from my eyes, and I quickly wiped them away. I rushed to sit at the table next to Ryan because they were coming into the dining room. I sat there smiling as Isiah and Ques walked into the room and stopped in their tracks. The smile I wore was quickly replaced by confusion. The two most important people in my life, besides my girls, didn't seem too happy to see me at all. They both wore a scowl on their face as they looked at me.

"Is no one happy to see me or something?" I asked, just to get the conversation going.

"How you expect us to be happy to see a liar?" Ques asked, sitting across from me.

"What is going on? Why is there so much hostility and tension in the room. Alani is finally home by the grace of God," Ryan said, trying to come to my defense.

"You sure it was by the grace of God, or was it because of you?" Isiah questioned Ryan.

"This is going all the way left. Obviously y'all have something to say, so just fucking say it." I was getting mad with the whole situation because it wasn't supposed to be like this.

"Y'all must think we are stupid or some shit. I can't even lie, you had me fooled for a minute. Talking about you wanted to handle this shit on your own. Did you not think I was going to find out that Enzo was the reason you were in jail? We bugged that nigga's house so we heard everything. Ryan, you a cold bitch for how you handled that," Isiah spat.

I looked on in shock as Isiah began to give me the run down. He told me all about how he had one of Ques' young dudes to follow Enzo around. He even knew about Ryan killing Enzo and getting rid of the body. I felt like shit as he yelled at me.

"Look Isiah, I didn't keep it away from you to hurt you. I did it because I felt as though the Feds would be watching you. I know how your attitude is and I didn't want you doing anything, then getting locked up too."

"I understand that, but you should have told me. Do you really think I would do something without thinking of all the consequences? I already knew my crew was being watched. I'm not new to this, I'm true to this baby girl. Harlem, you were wrong too for keeping it a secret. We are together, which means we don't hide shit from each other."

"I know but I was doing what was best for my friend, bae. You can't fault me for that," Harlem pouted.

"I'm not faulting you for that, which is why this is a warning. I don't want you keeping anything else from me, ight?"

"You got it daddy," she smiled.

"Ryan, I just want to say thanks for doing what you did. I know that shit couldn't have been easy for you," Isiah said, sitting at the table.

"Family over everything is how I look at it. He tried to bring one of our own down, and I couldn't let that happen. Ashes to ashes and dust to dust," she said.

Everyone was sitting at the table, but Ques. He was still staring at me from the doorway, giving me a cold look. A chill went through my spine as I looked at him. I excused myself from the table and walked right up to him. I didn't say anything, I just grabbed his hand and led him away.

Chapter Thirteen: Ques

It's not that I didn't know Alani was coming home, I just didn't think it would be so soon. Enzo's ass died just a few days ago. That lawyer we had played no fucking games. Seeing Alani sitting at the table like everything was cool pissed me off even more. Isiah was more understanding because that was her brother. Me on the other hand, I couldn't understand why she did shit the way she did. The girls still could've handled Enzo if Isiah and I knew what was going on. Alani just wanted to be in control like she always was. The only reason I allowed her to lead me away was because I wanted to see if she was going to apologize or try to justify the shit that she did.

If Alani tried to justify the bullshit, then there would be no us ever. Her justifying it would show that she still hasn't grown up. Now if she apologized, I would think about taking her ass back. I needed to see some type of growth in Alani if we were going to be in a relationship. The smart ass mouth and shit I was dealing with when we first got together wasn't going to fly now. I was growing up and maturing, so I need the same from her.

"Ques, I honestly just want to apologize for what I did. I could sit here and try to justify why I did what I did, but it wouldn't even matter. What matters is that I hurt you, and that was never my intention. I wanted nothing more than to protect you from ending up where I was. While sitting in jail, I had a lot of time to think, and the majority of the time was spent thinking about you. You came to me at a point in my life where I thought I wanted change, but I really wasn't ready for it, but I'm ready for it now. All I'm asking is that you don't cut me out of your life completely."

Alani was standing in front of me pleading her case with tears rolling down her eyes. She wasn't trying to wipe them either. She allowed them to flow freely, and I could appreciate that. It showed her vulnerable side, which was the side she tried to keep hidden all the time. I pulled her into my arms and just held her. I didn't say anything, I just held her in my arms the way I wanted to hold her for the last six weeks. I wanted to still be mad at Alani, but I couldn't. She had shown me growth in the words that she spoke to me. How could I still be mad when growth was the only thing I wanted from her?

"Stop crying, Chinky. It's okay ma," I told her. Hearing me call her Chinky, her head popped up. I wiped away her tears and gently kissed her on the lips.

"I'm still Chinky?" she questioned with a slight smile.

"You will always be Chinky to me, ma."

"I love you, Ques."

I brought my lips back to her mouth, kissing her so intensely that she couldn't deny that I felt the same. She jumped on me, wrapping her legs around my hips. I carried her to the bed and laid her down.

"Ques, I don't think we should do this just yet," she whispered.

"Why not?" I mumbled. My mouth was already hovering over her nipple, ready to attack.

"I just got out and I want our first time to be special."

"We already had sex before, so what you mean our first time, Alani?" All I wanted was to feel her walls wrapped around my dick. All this talking she was trying to do could be done right after I felt her.

"I'm talking about our first time since I've been out. I want it to be perfect. I don't want to have a quickie in my best friend's house."

"As long as it's the two of us, anything we do will be perfect. Just let me take you there, Chinky. You know you want me to."

Before she could respond, I bit her nipple through her shirt. Her back arched and a low moan escaped her mouth. I used my left hand to unsnap her bra and pulled it off with her shirt, exposing her breasts. I didn't know if it was because I haven't seen her in a while, but her breasts seemed bigger. I pushed them together, eagerly sucking on each of her hard nipples. Lani moaned as I bit and tugged at her nipples. I wanted to see how wet she was and if she missed daddy. I left her nipple alone so I could undo her jeans and slide them off her toned legs and thighs. I slipped her panties to the side and ran my fingers up and done her center.

"Yesss," she hissed.

"Fuck, you wet ma. You missed daddy?" I asked as I dipped my fingers in and out of her slowly.

She ignored me as she leaned up and kissed me. Her lips were soft and tasted like strawberry. I released her lips from mine, making lovingly trailed kisses down her chest, to her navel and then down to her thighs. I licked along her right thigh before bringing my tongue to her opening.

Her juices were pouring out, and I was ready to drink up. I greedily feasted on her kitty as if I hadn't eaten in months.

"Ques! Ahhhh yessss! That feels amazing!" Keep going daddy, keep going," she cooed as my tongue ran laps up and down her pussy lips.

I kept licking and sucking until she was bouncing off the bed, begging me to stop. From the way she was yelling, I had her right where I wanted her. I applied pressure to her clit as it swelled against my tongue. I sucked on her pussy with no remorse, aching to taste more of her juices.

"Jacques!" she cried as her body began to shake uncontrollably.

Like the starving nigga I was, I licked every drop, leaving her pussy glistening and dry.

I dived in her, not giving her warning. She screamed out in pleasure and I was sure the whole house heard her. Lani was wet and tight. I intertwined my fingers in hers and slowly stroked her middle. With each stroke, Lani bucked her hips, giving me the same sensation I was giving her. Whenever me and Lani had sex, I realized just how much I loved her. She was so helpless as her body gave in to my command. I grinded harder, rotating my hips in a clockwork motion.

"Ohhhhhh!"

"Cum for daddy! Cum on my dick ma," I demanded. Once again, her legs began to shake as we both hit our peeks. I bit into my bottom lip so I wouldn't scream like a bitch. Lani's pussy was suffocating me, and the feeling was insane.

We both laid there, basking in the smell of our sex. This was the first time I felt complete since Alani got locked up. I was just happy she was finally home with me where she belonged.

Chapter Fourteen: Harlem

"You sure you're not pregnant?" Isiah asked, coming into the bathroom with a bottle of water.

"No, I can't be pregnant. I have that IUD in me," I told him.

It's been about three days since Alani came home and I've been throwing up ever since. I thought it was a stomach virus or something, but Isiah kept pushing the pregnancy word down my throat.

"I keep telling you I got super sperm. You can say you're not pregnant all you want, but I know better. If you're still throwing up within the next couple of days, you're going to the doctor.

"Yes, daddy. Whatever you say," I sassed, rolling my eyes.

"What you got planned for the day?"

"Nothing much. Going to meet up with the girls and I guess just hang out," I shrugged.

"Since Lani been back home, that's all y'all do. Chill and hang out."

"There's not much else for us to do. It's not like we still working anymore."

"That's why you need to have my babies so they can keep you busy. I don't know what's the hold up anyway. We getting older, not younger. I'm about to be out of this street shit for good. The way I see it, now is as good as a time as any."

"I just don't know if I'm ready. I don't even know what I want to do with myself just yet. I think I want to open up some type of business, but I'm not sure."

"That doesn't mean we can't have a baby. We have more than enough money to have a baby and get you fifteen businesses. All you have to do is say the word, and your wish is my command."

"Isiah, there will be no babies until I get a ring on my finger. I know I grew up in the hood, but that doesn't mean I want to be the typical girl from the hood. I get a ring and your last name, then we can have all the babies you want. I'll be your baby making machine for life," I giggled.

"Don't say things you're not ready for ma. I might just pop up with a ring tomorrow and that means that IUD shit has to be out by the time our honeymoon comes around," he told me.

"I already told you what the deal was. Enough of this baby talk, it's making me nauseous. What are you doing today?"

"I have to go meet up with Demetri to talk about a few things."

"Wait, what? You're going to meet up with Ryan's Demetri?" I was shocked because the two never really talked. They would say wassup whenever they saw each other, but that was as far as it went.

"The hell you acting so shocked for? He's dating Ryan, which means he will be around often. Might as well get to know the guy, and he might be good for business."

"What kind of business?" I asked with an eyebrow raised.

"Business that doesn't concern you. Now be good and have dinner on the table by the time I get home," he said coming over to where I was in the bedroom and giving me a quick kiss.

"Dinner will be ready whenever I decide to cook it. I don't know who you think you're demanding," I giggled.

"You talking all that shit, let's see if your ass gets a ring."

"Don't play like that. Dinner will be ready at six!" I yelled after him.

"And I'll be at home by five thirty," he laughed.

I sat on the bed and turned on the TV, looking for something to watch. It was only eleven in the morning and I was sure Alani and Ryan were still booed up. I figured I would give them until one in the afternoon, then we were going out to lunch. Without thinking, I touched my stomach and could have sworn I felt a light kick. I chuckled to myself because I had to be going crazy. I had about a five percentage chance of getting pregnant while on the IUD. It would be crazy as hell if I actually was.

* * * *

"Do you remember when we came here and Alani went the hell off on Nisha because she was with Ques?" Ryan laughed as we were being seated at Junior's.

"How could I forget? That's when I knew she was really feeling him because she straight showed her ass for someone who wasn't even hers. Then she tried to pull out Tiffany on the bitch," I laughed.

"There isn't anything funny about that. I couldn't believe the way I acted," Alani said, shaking her head.

"He had you straight whipped before he even gave you the dick," I said.

"He did not have me sprung. The nigga was just on my radar. You know I love them then leave them," Lani smirked.

"Yeah, ight. Then why is his ass still around? It's okay to admit that you love that man. Harlem and I already know it," Ryan said.

"Y'all just don't understand how he makes me feel. It's like when I'm with him, I feel like a brand new me. I honestly feel like he was made for me. He was sculpted just for me, and I for him. I want to say we are soul mates, but it's so much deeper than that. That man really does make me better. He got me thinking about having kids and the whole nine. The nigga got me sprung and wrapped around his finger. Jacques is the real deal and he's it for me. That nigga got me on lock down and he don't even know it."

"Harlem, can you believe it, our little Alani is growing up," Ryan giggled and acted like she was wiping tears from her eyes.

"Y'all play way too much," Alani giggled.

"You know we are just playing with you. I'm happy you're finally opening yourself up to someone. Matter of fact, I'm proud of all of us. We each have men in our lives that love us down to our pissy draws," I smiled.

"I don't know about you, but my draws are not pissy."

"And neither are mine," Ryan chimed in.

"Y'all know what I mean," I laughed.

"How are things with you and Demetri?' Lani asked Ryan.

"I can tell he's still mad about the Enzo situation, but I don't know what else he wants me to say. The damage is done already."

"I think you just need to lay all your cards on the table. Tell him everything and then maybe he will get a better understanding. Honestly speaking, I thought the two of you were moving a little too fast, but the more I see y'all together, I realize the two of you are made for each other," I told Ryan.

Being in a relationship wasn't a cake walk. It was a lot of work, but as long as the person you're with is worth it, then all the work you have to put in doesn't matter. Ryan was so used to her being the person that had an attitude in the relationship that she didn't know how to deal with Demetri being upset. She wanted someone different than Enzo, and she got it. She would just have to put on her big girl panties and make it do what it do.

The three of us continued to chat and talk way into the late evening. When we were together, the time would fly. I couldn't imagine the three of us not being around each other and just talking about bullshit. Looking at my girls, I was proud of where each one of us were at today in our lives. We may not be where we are supposed to be, but we are a lot closer than where we were a couple months ago.

Chapter Fifteen: Isiah

"You sure you want to do this? I mean if you do, a nigga will be happy as hell, but I don't want you to compromise your beliefs and shit," I told Demetri as we stood around the pool table.

Ques, Demetri, and I decided to handle business at a pool hall around the way. I could have had the meeting at my warehouse or the crib, but I wanted to get out. Life has been stressful as hell, and now that everything was back to normal, all I wanted to do was breathe and enjoy life. I didn't want to worry about if my spots were making money or not. I damn sure didn't want to worry about having to look over my shoulder. I was ready to be done with the whole drug shit. I was ready to have a wife and kids. In other words, a nigga was ready to go all the way legit. I had a couple of businesses, but none of them were big enough to help clean up my money. I didn't want nothing coming to bite me in the ass. When I got out, I was ready to be out for good. Wasn't going to be cell bars or a casket for me. I wanted the white picket fence and shit. I was ready to be on my real grown man shit, and me being here meeting with Demetri was the first step in the right direction for me.

"I don't do shit that I don't want to do, and I damn sure don't do shit that's not profitable for me," Demetri said.

"We not trying to make it seem like you don't know what you're doing, we just want to make sure you are a hundred percent on board. Once we start this shit, there ain't no going back," Ques told him.

"Nigga," Demetri chuckled, "I may not be a street nigga, but trust me, I'm street nigga. My moms cooks up your dope. I know what I'm doing. If I say I'm going to help you clean up your money, then that's what I'm going to do. No need to ask me if I'm sure a thousand times because I don't say shit unless I'm sure of the move I'm making."

"Ight nigga, I feel you," I told him.

"Nigga, you getting deep and shit," Ques laughed.

"Nah, not even. Just want y'all to know that I'm serious."

"Your word is your bond, so I'm straight." We dapped each other up like it was nothing, and continued to play pool.

Shit, with Demetri helping us clean up this money, I was ready to take things to the next level. I wanted a baby, and Harlem wanted a wedding. I was all for giving my baby what she wanted, I was just going to do it my way and when I was ready. But best believe when a nigga did it, I was going to do it big.

* * * *

"Honey, I'm home!" I yelled, walking into the house.

"You don't need to yell," Harlem said, coming towards the front door with a bottle of water in her hand. She was rocking a tank top with a pair of my boxers. The boxers clung to her ass, making my dick hard on sight.

"Damn, I said have dinner on the table when I got home, not have an attitude," I grabbed her into my arms, leading the way into the kitchen.

"I don't have an attitude, I'm just tired," she sighed.

"Yeah, I bet you are. What you do today?"

"Nothing really, chilled with the girls and had lunch. Then I came home whipped up some tacos and been chilling ever since," Harlem smiled.

"Oh ight," I told her, sitting at the table waiting for her to bring me my plate of food.

"How was the meeting?" she asked. Harlem placed my plate in front of me, then went over to the fridge, pulling out some juice. She then got me a cup with ice and sat next to me, pouring some juice in my cup. That's why I loved this girl. No matter what it was, she always made sure that I was straight.

"The meeting was cool. In the next six months or so, things are really about to change for us."

"I hope it's a good change."

"Of course it's a good change. The only way we can go from here is up baby girl. Now go lay down and I'll be up to run you some bath water."

"Okay," she kissed me on the cheek and I slapped her on the ass before she walked away.

Harlem was really a blessing. She had always been around, but to have her as my girl was something special. The day I found out about her having a crush on me was the day I really started living. She just made everything better for me. She was a nigga's safe haven. I wanted to be mad with her about the whole Enzo situation, but I couldn't even do it because she had my best interest at heart. She knew that if I would've found out, he would've be dead on sight.

That shit with Enzo was a whole different story. I wasn't one to get into my feelings or nothing, but that shit really fucked me up. He was like a brother to me and he went and did some snake shit. I wish I could have been there because I would've asked his bitch ass why he did it. I never showed him nothing but love and he still had larceny in his heart. I saved him from a couple of beat downs and he repays me by getting my sister locked up. Growing up, I was always on some we shit. I guess that nigga was on that I shit.

I wasn't going to sweat it too much. Losing a friend hurts, but when you have a whole family that has your back through thick and thin, the shit don't even matter. Everyone that was supposed to be in my life, is in my life. Anyone that isn't got what they deserve; it was as simple as that for me.

Chapter Sixteen: Ryan

After lunch with the girls, I came straight home to cook dinner for Demetri. I wasn't hungry, but I wanted to do something nice for him. We have been on the rocks lately and I couldn't stand it. The whole silent treatment was new to me because I was usually the one giving the silent treatment. I knew he was upset, but I honestly thought he was dragging the whole situation. He claimed he wasn't mad, but he wasn't really fucking with me. I was hoping the dinner would fix things between us, but it didn't because he never came back to my house.

To say I was pissed wouldn't even justify my true feelings. I didn't even bother to try calling because I wasn't going to be one of those girls again. I went through the emotions with Enzo and I wasn't about to go through them again with Demetri. I was starting to think the whole relationship thing wasn't for me. Enzo was my first everything and that ended up being shit. Then Demetri comes into my life and I start to think he is the one, but he starts acting up too. Maybe the problem wasn't the men I choose, but maybe the problem was me. As quickly as that thought came, it left. I damn sure wasn't the problem. There wasn't anything wrong with me; they had to be the problem.

I rolled out of bed, not really having much to do. I planned on staying in the house and just cuddling up with my blanket. I jumped in the shower, washed up, brushed my teeth and all that good stuff, then got out. With my robe covering my body, I walked towards the kitchen to make me a cup of hot chocolate. The food from last night was still out because I fell asleep trying to wait for Demetri to come over. I emptied out all of the pots, watching the food I cooked go to waste. Once the pots were empty, I sat them in the sink, allowing them to soak. I made my hot chocolate, adding a couple of marshmallows, and was about to head back to my bedroom when I heard my front door open.

To my knowledge, no one had a key to my house expect for my girls, and they always called before just coming over. I rushed into the kitchen, sitting my hot chocolate down and grabbing one of the many pistols I had stashed all around my house. I walked back towards the front door with my pistol raised, only to be greeted by Demetri.

"The fuck you doing with a gun, Ryan?" he barked. His eyes were cold, leading me to believe the nigga still had an attitude.

I sucked my teeth, ignored his question, went back to hide my pistol and grabbed my hot chocolate. I walked right passed him like he wasn't even there and went into my bedroom. I snuggled up in my covers on my bed and turned on the TV. I didn't bother flicking through the channels because nothing is ever on. Instead, I went to on demand to find a good movie to watch. I wasn't in my bed for even a good five minutes before Demetri came busting into my room.

"Ryan, don't get fucked up in this muthafucker. When I talk to you, you answer. We not on that kids shit. Ight?"

"Oh, you're one to talk. You have been ignoring me for weeks over some bullshit. But we not on that kid shit, right?" I spat.

"If you sleeping with another nigga is bullshit, then let me go sleep with another chick so we can be on that bullshit together."

"Don't talk that slick shit to me. Go sleep with another bitch if you want to. I promise your ass won't wake up to see tomorrow."

"The fuck are you talking about? You threatening me now and shit? Ryan, who the fuck are you?"

For some strange reason, that question caught me a little off guard. Did he really want to know who I was or was he just trying to say some bullshit?

"Demetri, what the hell are you talking about?" I was confused, but I refused to let him get the last word in when he was in the wrong.

"You know exactly what I'm talking about. When I first met you, you were feisty, but you had this type of innocence about you. Now it just seems like you switched up on a nigga."

"You knew I was into some street shit when you first met me. Your mother told you I was the boss when you met me. Who you're getting right now is me, and if you can't handle it, then maybe you should step and leave my key that I didn't even know you had."

"Of course you didn't know I had your key because you haven't been paying attention to shit. No lie, since you found out that fuck nigga was the reason Lani was in jail, you been all about them. Then Alani get out and it's still all about them."

"Wait, are you mad because I don't give you enough attention?"

"Nah, I'm mad because your ass has a one track mind. But it's cool though, because this is who you are and if I'm not okay with it then I should step, right?"

"Demetri, wait!" I yelled. He turned to walk away and as bad as I wanted him to leave, I just couldn't let him walk away from me.

"Wait for what? I'm not fucking with you no more, Ryan. You're not the chick I thought you were."

"Just talk to me, damn. You say we not on no kid shit, but you're trying to run away instead of talking about our problems. Nothing is going to get solved like that." I had to use his own words against him because I didn't know what else to say.

"Then get to talking, ma."

I reached over, grabbing my hot chocolate, taking a couple of sips to buy me some time. When I said we needed to talk, I assumed that he would tell me what his issue was, then I would say what I needed to say. I didn't think he was going to want me to talk first.

"Demetri, look, I don't know what you want me to say."

"That's the problem. You shouldn't have to think about what I want you to say, you should just tell me the truth. Tell me what's in your heart; it's as simple as that baby girl. You're the only one making it harder than what it has to be."

"Fine, you want me to speak from the heart, then here it goes. Enzo was my first everything, but more importantly, he was my first love. I loved him so deep that I allowed him to treat me any type of way. I can sit here and say it's because I didn't know my worth, but that would be a lie. I know exactly what I deserve and I know my worth. But love has a funny way of making you forget all of that. For so long, Enzo is the only man I've known on a sexual, spiritual, and mental level. I put my all into the relationship and I couldn't fathom Enzo being with anyone else, so I put up with his bullshit. Finding out he was sleeping with your sister and her baby was supposed to be his, was the last straw. I was over it and at the same time, it changed something in me. I refused to be that same woman I was with him. I refused to let love consume me so much that I forget that my worth comes first. Things with you happened really fast, and at first, you were supposed to be a rebound. Somehow, I allowed myself to become engulfed with you. You became something my body craved for, and my mind demanded your conversation."

"I hear all of that you're saying, and trust me when I tell you that I understand. What I don't get is why you would sleep with a nigga that caused you so much pain when your mind and body wanted me."

"I wasn't supposed to sleep with him, that wasn't part of the plan."

"What plan Ryan?"

"As you know, Enzo was the reason Alani was in jail. So the only way to get her out was to eliminate the problem. I was just supposed to get close to Enzo so that he would trust me again. A conversation we were having ended up turning into sex. I didn't enjoy the sex or anything, but it still shouldn't have happened."

"Wait, hold up, you killed Enzo?" Demetri asked laughing. I was taken aback by his laughter because I didn't say anything funny.

"Did I miss the joke or something?"

"Ma, you're not no killer. I can kill a nigga before you would."

"Demetri, don't let the cute face fool you. What did you think Alani, Harlem, and I did? We damn sure wasn't pushing no weight."

"I thought y'all was transporting drugs or some shit. Killing damn sure wasn't on my list of jobs you did."

"Trust, me and my girls are the deadliest females you would ever meet."

"Damn, ma. I guess I can understand, but that still doesn't explain why you kept me on the back burner. Like a nigga was hurt finding out you slept with that nigga. That should mean something to you because my feelings don't get hurt. Anyway, I expected you to try and fix things between us, but instead, you allowed me to walk around here like you weren't even around. You dead ass fought over that weak minded nigga, but didn't even try to get me to talk to you. You dead ass let me do me."

"I didn't fight for you because I figured you had steam to blow off. You told me I was on my own. I never seen a dude handle the situation the way you handled it, so I didn't know how to go about it. You not talking to me had me fucked up and I wanted to fix things, I just didn't know how to step to you."

"There was no real way you needed to step to me. All you had to do was tell me to get out my feelings and shit would have been sweet. Like I told yo ass that night, I'm man enough to deal with your fuck ups. I'm not these other dudes out here that's going to put they hands on a chick because she fucked up. I have done my fair share of dirt in the past, so I'm not perfect, and I don't expect you to be either. You made a mistake, and even though I had to drag the truth out of you, I respect it. Like I done told you before, don't let that shit happen again because once is a mistake, twice is taking advantage," he said.

"I understand, but quick question." I was glad we cleared the air some, but I still wanted to know where his ass was last night.

"Wassup?"

"Where were you last night? I cooked dinner and everything for us, but you never came over."

"First off, how was I supposed to know you cooked dinner? Did you pick up the phone to call or text me to come over? Nah, you just assumed I was coming over like I usually do. That's your problem, you assume too much instead of saying what you really want. But to answer your question, I was at my mom's house packing up the little bit of stuff I have there and checking on my sister."

"Packing up your stuff for what?"

"I have to get ready to go back up state."

"You're leaving me?" I pouted. I have been trying to get him to move down here to the city, but the nigga always said we'll see. I didn't know what him moving back upstate meant for our relationship.

"Yeah, I have some things I need to take care of. I'll be back though."

"I just don't understand why you can't move down here," I mumbled.

"Yo, what you just say? If you have something to say, put some bass in your voice ma," he smirked, coming over to the bed and jumping on top of me.

"I said I don't understand why you just won't move out here."

"The city life isn't for me ma. I come down here to check on my family and that's it."

"Then what about us?" I asked, feeling some type of way.

"You can always move upstate with me. What's really left for you in the city? I'm sure you can still kill people upstate."

"I don't kill people anymore smart ass, but my family is down here. Isiah, Ques, Alani, Harlem, and I may not be blood, but they are my family."

"They can always come visit us and you can always go visit them. Sometimes you have to do what's best for you and not think about how it's going to affect other people. I would love if you came upstate with me, but if you decided to stay here, then I'm sure we can make it work."

"You would do that for me?" I asked in shock.

"Do what for you?"

"Make the long distance relationship work?"

"Ryan, I would catch the moon and the stars if it means I get to be with you. Distance isn't a thing when love is involved," he said kissing me.

I kissed him back, but then it hit me; he had just said he loved me. I wasn't going to say anything about it because I didn't want to mess up the moment. However, a bitch was smiling on the inside. The kissing turned into moans and you know what that means. Demetri was about to give me that good dick that puts me to sleep. I put me moving upstate to the back of my mind because I wasn't ready to think about that just yet. For the mean time in between time, I was going to enjoy this loving my baby was giving me. He was my happiness and so much more. Enzo's fuck up with Ciara was my blessing in disguise.

Chapter Seventeen: Ques

"Ques, how am I supposed to know how I need to dress if you're not telling me where we are going?" Chinky complained. "You know I don't like surprises anyway."

"Do you ever just shut up and go with the flow, damn," I spat.

I woke Chinky up early this morning because I had a surprise for her ass. First, she was complaining about getting up early, and now she was complaining about not knowing what to wear. Alani was my everything, but she got on my fucking nerves sometimes. Since she's been home, we haven't really been outside of the house together. We have been making up for lost time, if you know what I mean.

"You are so disrespectful. I don't even know why I'm with your ugly ass," she walked past me, bumping into me a little.

"You with me because you don't have a fucking choice. No other dude would put up with you and your reckless ass mouth. You keep running it and I'm going to put something long and hard in that shit."

"You're so fucking nasty, Jacques," she rolled her eyes and I smacked her on the ass.

"Yeah, whatever. You like that nasty shit," I told her.

"On another note, I been staying low because I wanted things to die down, but I'm ready to make my presence known to Silver. I owe her ass a buck fifty and bullet to the dome."

The only people that know about me handling Silver, was Isiah and Demetri. I wanted to keep it that way, but I knew Alani wasn't going to let the shit go.

"That shit is already taken care of," I told her.

"What do you mean it's already taken care of? Who killed her ass?"

"It doesn't matter who did it, all that matters is that it's handled." I walked past her and went into the bathroom to brush my teeth. I should've locked the door behind me because not even a minute later, she waltzed in the bathroom, popping shit. I continued brushing my teeth as she went on and on about how she wanted to be the one to kill her and all this other bullshit I wasn't interested in. I finished brushing my teeth and her ass was still going.

"Chinky, go sit your little ass down somewhere and shut up. I killed the bitch because she deserved to die. Did you really think her ass would still be around by the time you got out? You should be saying thank you instead of bitching."

"What do you mean I should be saying thank you? That bitch tried to kill me, so I should've been the one to end her life. I don't understand why that is so hard for you to understand."

"Ight, if we are looking at it like that, then I should've been the one to kill Enzo since he took you away from me and had you acting dumb as hell."

"That's different," she tried to explain, but I cut her little ass off.

"Ain't nothing different about that shit. Your problem is that you try to be in control of everything. Alani, you don't run shit, and the faster you realize that, the better off me and you will be. Last time I checked, I was the one with the dick hanging between my legs. For real Alani, just chill and let me drive the car. You hold down the passenger seat with Tiffany and pull the trigger when I need you to."

"Okay, daddy," she purred, coming and kissing me on the cheek. I slapped her on the ass and told her to hurry up so we could go. I left out the bedroom and went into the living room.

Alani still got on my fucking nerves, but she has also chilled out a lot. She still had her moments where she thought she was boss, but it wasn't nothing for me to put that to rest. Just like she had to learn to let me lead, I had to learn that she wasn't going to change overnight. It was going to take time, but as long as I saw growth, I didn't mind waiting on her ass. I haven't told her that I was planning on getting out of the game just yet. A part of me was a little nervous about telling her because I didn't know how she was going to take it. She damn near cried when we wanted her to get out. Chinky wasn't like the regular chicks, she thrived from hearing about the street shit. I had more to offer than just the thug mentality though. I just hoped she would be on board with some of the plans I had in store for us.

"Okay, I'm ready," Alani said, standing in front of me.

I looked her over and I could have sworn she was getting thicker. She was thick before she went to jail, but when she came out, she was a brick house. Now it seemed as though her hips were still spreading. She had on a pair of black skinny jeans that clung to her hips for dear life. She wore a plain black t-shirt with an olive green and black leather jacket. A pair of thigh high heels adorned her feet, giving her a couple of inches in height. Her hair was pulled back in a simple pony tail.

"Ma, you killing it. I may have to take your ass out to show you off with the way you looking," I told her, licking my lips.

"I thought we were going out. Damn it, Ques. Let me go change real quick. I feel like I'm overdressed," she said, ready to walk off. I grabbed on to her hips, holding her in place.

I stood up, towering over her little frame. She was beautiful in every sense of the word. She didn't have on any make up, and could still kill every chick she walked passed.

"You look fine, ma. Now let's go," I kissed her, grabbing my keys and jacket and heading out the door.

I helped her into the car, then jumped inside. I wanted to take my bike, but it was too cold for that and I didn't need Chinky getting sick. Once I got in, I turned the radio up so Alani wouldn't be able to ask me any questions. Chinky could cook her ass off, but the stuff she baked was out of this world. I purchased her the bakery the night she got locked up. When she cut a nigga off, I had plans to sell it, but the man in me wouldn't allow me to. Regardless of if Alani and I were together or not, I believed in her. Baking was something that she loved, but for some reason, she never took seriously. It could have been because of all the street shit she was involved in, but that was a thing of the past now. I wanted her to start thinking on a more legitimate level. This bakery was just going to be the start of her empire.

* * * *

"So you made me get out of my bed to come see a building?"

"What I tell you about that complaining shit? Just shut up and come inside please. You always running your mouth and you don't even know what the hell you be talking about half the time," I grabbed her hand, unlocked the front door and pushed her ass inside.

"You didn't have to push me," she sassed.

"Would you feel better if I would have thrown your ass inside?' I laughed.

"Stop playing and tell me what we are doing here Jacques."

I ignored her ass and hit the lights. Above her head there was a banner that said 'Alani would you'. She turned towards me with nervousness and uncertainty written all over her face.

"Ques, what is this? I hope you're not going to propose to me because I don't think we are ready for that. Not even we, I'm not ready for that. I love you and I'm in love with you, but marriage is a big step. We haven't even been dating for long. We still have a lot to work on in our relationship. Please don't tell me you're going to ask me to marry you because I would hate to break your heart and tell you no. Ques, say something damn it," she said all in one breath.

I chuckled a little because Alani was really fucking crazy. She just did all that talking and everything she said was straight assumptions. I wasn't dumb enough to ask Alani to marry me because anyone could see that we weren't ready for that. Alani wasn't going anywhere anyway, so we had all the time in the world to get married.

"This is what I'm talking about, Chinky. You're always trying to be in control of a situation and you don't even know what's going on. If you would've just came in here and let me speak, then your ass wouldn't be rambling on about how we aren't ready to get married. Just like you, I have a lot of growing up to do and right now, I'm not the man I want you to marry."

"Then what is this Ques?" she asked with a look of relief.

"Chinky, I see so much potential in you that it's crazy. I think I see your potential more than you see it in yourself. Anything you put your mind to, you excel in, and that's something not a lot of people can do. I see the way your face lights up whenever you're baking. I knew that if I would've brought this idea to you, your stubborn ass would have come up with excuses on why it wouldn't have worked. You have told me more times than I can count how much you love it, so I did what any real dude would do. I bought you this place so it can be your bakery. Killing niggas and shit was a means to an end for you. You did it because you wanted fast money. Now you have more than enough money and you no longer need to do it. Killing is beneath you and I refuse to allow you to partake in anything that isn't on your level. You have the opportunity to make money doing something that you love and that's rare, because not a lot of people get that chance."

"Okay, but what does the banner mean?"

"Alani, will you take this bakery and turn it into something that you can be proud of which will ultimately make me proud of you? Alani, will you promise to do everything in your power to become the woman that you are destined to be? Alani, will you continue to flaunt your flaws because those are the things I love about you the most? If you say yes to all the things I'm asking you, then I will make you a couple of promises of my own."

"Yes," she cried, smiling through the tears.

"Then I promise to never leave your side no matter the storm. I promise to make sure that you always have a shoulder to lean on when you feel like everything is becoming too much. I promise to help you better yourself as a woman. I promise to be the man that will wipe your tears away instead of causing them. I promise to make sure all of our good times waiver the bad. I promise that you will adorn my last name. I promise that I will love you unconditionally through thick and thin. I promise that I will be the dude you want and deserve. Most importantly, I promise to be that nigga that's down to ride to the very end."

I walked closer to her, grabbing her hands and sealing my promise with a kiss. I then pulled away, slipped a ring out of my pocket and put it on her ring finger.

"Oh my God, Jacques!" she squealed.

"This isn't an engagement ring, it's a promise ring. As long as you wear this ring, everything I promised you will become your future. It's me and you until the end, Chinky. I see nothing but you in my future, and that's a dope ass future if you ask me."

Tears were dropping on the fancy intense yellow diamond halo ring I got her. The ring was one of a kind. The 18k yellow gold ring was showcased with a breathtaking yellow radiant cut diamond, which was accented by a halo of diamonds. The ring cost me about fifty thousand, which wasn't nothing to me. It was just a promise ring, so I went big without going too big. When it was time to propose to her, best believe she was going to have a mini glacier on her hand.

"I don't even know what to say, Ques. I can't believe you did all of this for me."

"I would do anything for you if it meant you would have that beautiful smile on your face. All I want in this life of sin is you."

"I love you so much," she smiled, burying her face in my chest.

"I love you too, ma."

I held her for what felt like an eternity, but I didn't care because I had her. I probably sound soft as fuck, but I didn't care. Chinky was my world and I was going to let her know and show her that every day, as long as there was air in my body. For her, I would be as soft as she wanted me to be. A nigga wasn't pussy whipped or nothing. It just so happened I found love when I met Alani, and she found a rider when she started fucking with me.

Chapter Eighteen: Harlem

Ryan and I were helping Alani pack up her stuff so she could move in with Ques, and I could move in with Isiah. I thought I would never see the day Alani moved in with a dude, but I couldn't have been happier for her. She told us all about how Ques told her about the bakery and gave her the promise ring. I was truly happy for my girl because she deserved everything she was getting and more.

"That's why no one could find your ass over the weekend. You were too busy busting it open for a real nigga," Ryan giggled, doing a little dance, causing the rest of us to laugh.

"We weren't even having sex. Sex isn't the only thing we do. Maybe you should get some because that seems to be the only thing your mind is on," Lani laughed.

"Man, it's only been three days since Demetri left and I'm going through withdrawals. This shit is so unnatural. Whenever we FaceTime, we have to have cybersex because my ass be horny as hell," Ryan confessed.

"You some type of freaky," I laughed.

"Don't knock it until you try it. The shit gives me a high."

"I will not be trying that no time soon. I would hate for someone to hack my iPhone in the middle of me busting a nut," Lani said.

"Who the hell is going to hack your phone in the middle of your FaceTime call?" I asked, laughing my ass off. Alani was always saying some next shit.

"Y'all can laugh all you want, but technology is so advanced now a days that it's crazy. Keep having your little cybersex, and when I see the shit on Facebook, I'll make sure to tag your ass."

"Girl, shut up. No one's video is going to end up on Facebook," Ryan giggled.

"I'm hungry as hell," I said, really to myself.

I knew the reason why I was hungry, but I didn't want anyone else to know. Curiosity got the best of me so I finally took a pregnancy test. I ended up taking about four because I didn't believe the results on the first one. But three sticks later, I got the same results. I was indeed pregnant. Isiah didn't know yet because I wasn't ready to tell him. It's not that I didn't want him to know, I just had to wrap my head around it first. It's not like I wasn't careful, I just so happened to be a part of the five percent. I honestly didn't think that five percent existed. I always thought it was something people said so kids wouldn't have sex.

"Me too, what y'all want to eat?" Ryan asked.

"I'm not eating anything because that's only going to slow us down. I'm trying to beat Ques to the house. If I carry my stuff inside, that means he can put it away," Alani giggled.

"You are so lazy," I told her.

"Call it what you want. I don't feel like putting this stuff away. He wants me to move in, then the least he could do is help."

"I hear that one. Demetri wants me to move upstate with him, but I'm just not sure if I'm ready to leave New York City," Ryan said.

"Why not? What's left in New York for you?" Alani shrugged.

"Lani!" I yelled, slapping her on the arm.

"What?" she asked back.

"You don't have to be so insensitive, you know. Damn."

"I'm not being insensitive, I'm being truthful. There is nothing keeping her from moving to be with the man that she loves."

"Y'all are here. We have never been separated since we became friends," Ryan said.

"I understand that Ryan, but you can't use that as an excuse. No matter where you go, we will always be here for you because we are more than friends, we are sisters. At some point, you have to stop and live for yourself. Before, you were living for Enzo and doing what makes him happy. Now, you are trying to live for me and Harlem. We appreciate it, but we don't need you to."

"Look at you, sounding all deep and shit," I joked, trying to lighten the mood.

Alani was right with everything she said. Ryan was always the one that was trying to make sure everyone was okay. She literally put everyone else before herself.

"I'm not trying to live for y'all, I swear I'm not. I just don't feel right moving and not knowing anyone out there. What if Demetri and I get into it, where am I supposed to go?"

"You're not supposed to go anywhere. You are grown. Running away from your problems isn't going to fix anything. You arc going to stay there and fix the shit, then go on like the happy couple you are," I told her.

"I just don't know. He said that even if I don't move, we can still be together."

"How the hell is that supposed to work?" Alani asked, taking the words right out of my mouth.

"We can have a long distance relationship," Ryan said.

"Let me put you up on game right quick. He only said that because he wants to make you happy. Deep down, that isn't what he wants. Demetri cares about you so much that he would put his own happiness aside just so you can be comfortable. When are you going to put your happiness aside so he can comfortable?" I asked her.

"Shit, look at it this way, the nigga has only been gone for three days and you already having withdrawals without him. How do you expect to feel when he's gone for months?" Alani questioned.

"I can always go up there and visit him when he can't come visit me."

"For all of that, you might as well just move up there. Ryan, stop being dumb. We all know, including you, that you moving upstate with Demetri is a good idea."

"I know. I'm just scared."

"There is no reason to be scared, love. Of course a relationship isn't an easy thing, but nothing worth having is easy, and what's easy isn't worth having," Alani explained to her.

"Okay, I don't know what Ques is doing to you, but you are getting way too deep for me. Does that nigga have you watching Dr. Phil or some shit?" I laughed.

"No bitch, it's called maturity. While in jail, I was reading a lot of self-help books and they helped me realize that I act the way I do because of the resentment I have for my mother. I'm really just trying to be a better me for myself and Ques."

"Well shit, if Alani can grow up, maybe I do need to make that move," Ryan joked.

"You need to make that move. It'll just be the start of something beautiful," I told her.

"I'll think about it. I'm starting to feel like you bitches want me to leave," she pouted.

"It's not that we want you to leave, we just want the best for you. From what I can see, Demetri is what's best for you," Alani said.

"I agree with Dr. Alani."

"I can't fucking stand you bitches. Y'all over here joking on me and shit, but don't let the growth fool you. I still carry Tiffany everywhere I go." Alani went in her pocket, on the right side of her sweats, and pulled out Tiffany.

"I'ma have to tell Ques to take that shit from you, especially once you open that bakery. We all know you're not people friendly and we don't need, nor want, you pulling Tiffany out on your customers," Ryan said.

"I owe both of you a couple of bullets. Keep playing with me if you want to," Alani laughed, waving her gun around.

We finished packing up and loaded up the U-Haul Alani rented. Ryan left out with Alani to help her bring the stuff in Ques' house. I stayed behind because I started to feel a little sick. I made a doctor's appointment for Wednesday. It was only Monday, so I still had a couple of days to tell Isiah about the baby. I went and laid down for a little while. Before I drifted to sleep, Isiah sent me a text saying we were having movie night tonight and to order some Chinese food. I rolled my eyes at the text, but told him to tell me when he was ten minutes away. I wasn't in the mood for movies or Chinese food, but if it would make Isiah happy, then I was all down for it.

* * * *

"Harlem, wake up ma," I heard Isiah call out. I tried to sit up, but my body was too tired to move. I wiped the sleep from my eyes and the drool from my mouth before opening my eyes and seeing Isiah standing in the bedroom doorway.

"I tired to call you so you could order the food, but you didn't answer. You ight?"

"Yeah, I'm just a little tired. What you want to eat? I'll order the food now," I told him.

"Shrimp and broccoli with a side of white rice and some shrimp Lo Mein, no veggies. Get a couple of chicken wings too and tell them to put extra hot sauce in the bag. I've been craving fried chicken all day." He walked out the room and I giggled a little. I guess he was getting my pregnancy cravings because my ass hasn't craved a damn thing.

I got out of bed and searched for my phone. I found it and quickly put in our order. When I was done, I placed Isiah's pajamas on the bed so he could change out of his street clothes. I hated when he would come in from outside and lounge around the house in his street clothes. I then ran him a shower so he could really relax when we watched movies.

"I was just about to turn on the shower so I could jump in before the food came," he said, coming back in the room.

"I figured that, so I got it started for you. The food should be here within the next thirty minutes, so don't take too long. I'll be in the kitchen making lemonade. Pick a comedy movie because I'm not in the mood for nothing scary."

Scary movies and thrillers were our favorite movies, but I didn't think I could stomach someone getting killed tonight. I gave Isiah a quick kiss before going to make the lemonade. After I finished making the fresh lemonade, the doorbell was ringing. I was surprised because the food came a lot faster than it was supposed to. I brought the food upstairs, then came back into the kitchen to get us some trays, plates, and cups with ice. After sitting all of that down in the bedroom, I had to run back to the kitchen one last time because I forgot to grab the lemonade.

"Look at you, got everything set up like we eating in a five-star restaurant or something," Isiah smiled, coming out of the bathroom with a towel wrapped below his waist.

"Boy, shut up and put some clothes on. You know how you get when your food gets cold."

While he got dressed, I fixed both of our plates of food. I was hungry as hell and the smell of the food was intoxicating. I couldn't wait to dig in and stuff my face.

"You wanna watch *Think Like a Man Too?*" Isiah asked, getting on the bed.

"Sure," I smiled. I loved any movie with Kevin Hart in it because he was funny as hell. I guess that was the only option he had, since he was so short.

Isiah started the movie and we sat back, eating our food and watching the movie. I loved when we did things like this because it was just simple. We didn't have to be overly dressed or anything like that. We were just comfortable and enjoying each other's company. Half way through the movie, and on my second plate of food, my stomach started to act up. I could feel everything I just ate ready to come pouring out of my mouth. I told Isiah to pause the movie, then I rushed out of the room. I made it to the toilet just in time to pour my dinner in the toilet. I was pissed off because I assumed morning sickness was only meant for the morning. That obviously wasn't the case with my child. I would throw up all throughout the day, and the shit was annoying as hell. It was so bad I had to carry a toothbrush and toothpaste around in my bag whenever I went out.

"You need me to hold your hair back," Isiah laughed, coming into the bathroom.

"Ha ha ha, very funny," I told him. I wiped my mouth with the sleeve of my shirt before trying to get off the floor. Isiah reached out to help me, but I didn't want his help. This shit was his fault anyway, and I didn't want him touching me.

"Harlem, chill the fuck out 'cause I didn't do nothing to you. If your ass wasn't in denial about being pregnant, then we could find something for the nausea."

I just looked at him and rolled my eyes. "I'm not stupid, Isiah. I know this is exactly what you wanted. All you want me to be is barefoot and pregnant, stuck in the house, taking care of your twenty kids." I was honestly just saying shit to try to make him feel bad.

"Where the hell did you get that from? We don't live in the eighteen hundreds; no one wants your ass barefoot and pregnant. I don't even want twenty kids. One would be more than enough for me. You bugging ma," he asked, walking away then coming right back. "Here, I'm tired of your ass being in denial," he threw a bag of pregnancy tests at me, then walked out the room. I left them shits right there on the floor and followed him out of the bathroom.

"Harlem, what are you following me for? If you want to pee out here, that's cool, but know you will be the one cleaning it up."

"How are you just going to throw pregnancy tests at me like I wasn't just throwing up? Do you even care that I don't feel good?"

"That was a stupid ass question. I'm not even going to dignify that with an answer. Go pee on the stick, Harlem." He got back on the bed and picked up his plate of food. I looked on in disbelief at the way he was acting so nonchalantly.

"So you really don't care!"

"Harlem, you're the one making it harder than what it is. All you have to do is take the test, then we can take it from there. But instead of doing that, you'd rather argue about you being barefoot. Come on, the fuck you stalling for? We both know you're carrying my seed. I just bought the test so you could see the proof and get happy about the situation."

"Fine, you want me to take the test, then I'll take the damn tests," I stormed out of the bedroom, heading to the bathroom.

I slammed the door behind me for dramatic effect. I already knew I was pregnant, so there was really no need for me to take these test. I made a big deal about it because Isiah was getting what he wanted and I wasn't. Call me selfish, or a baby, but I didn't care. I took one of the test out the package, peed on it, then sat it on the back of the toilet. While I waited for the positive sign to appear, I brushed my teeth and rinsed my mouth with mouthwash. By the time I was done, the test was ready. I picked it up and walked out of the bathroom and back into the bedroom.

"So wassup, we pregnant or nah?" Isiah smiled. If I was closer to him, I would have wiped the smile right off his face.

Instead of being violent, I threw the test at Isiah, hitting him on the lip.

"Come on, Harlem. That's fucking nasty. It has your pee on it. I don't want that on my damn lip." I ignored his little bitch fit, grabbed my plate of food, and headed out the room. I sat in the kitchen, finishing up my food. It tasted better now than what it did earlier. When I was done, I cleaned my plate and just sat around. I was waiting for Isiah to come downstairs, happy as hell about the results. Twenty minutes passed and there was still no Isiah. I went back upstairs to find him sitting at the bed, staring at the test.

"You wanna know the results?" he asked, looking at me.

"I already know."

"So wassup, how you feel?"

"Why don't you tell me how you feel? You're the one sitting there all in shock and shit," I told him. I walked in the room and closed the door behind me. I climbed on the bed, sitting Indian style.

"I can't be happy about something if the love of my life isn't feeling it. "

"It's not that I'm not feeling it, it's just that I didn't think things were going to end up like this. It was supposed to be marriage, then the baby carriage. It said so in the song," I pouted.

"You are such a baby. Come here," Isiah reached out to me and I dove into his arms. "Things don't always go as planned, and that's okay. Since when have you known me to follow the rules anyway. I do what the fuck I want," he laughed.

"This is different. This is a real human that we have to take care of."

"I know, and we got this. When we are together, we are unstoppable. There is nothing in this world that we can't handle. Baby, I got you and my baby, so don't even trip. This was all part of a plan that's bigger than us. I got you for whatever ma."

"I know you do," I smiled and cuddled into his chest.

There was nothing more for me to say because Isiah was right. Things don't always happen the way I want them to, so the only thing I could do was roll with the punches. But I did know one thing, my ring better had been coming soon… real soon.

Chapter Nineteen: Demetri

I know y'all was waiting for me to make my presence known, well here I am. A lot of y'all probably thought I was on some sneak shit when I started fucking with Ryan, but that wasn't the case. Ryan is fine as hell, so of course I was going to push up on her, even though her old dude was fucking with my sister. That whole situation was crazy and I chewed my sister out for that shit. I told my moms on numerous occasions to let her come stay with me because she didn't need to be around the drug shit. My moms didn't want to listen to me, and now Ciara was pregnant by a nigga who was in jail. She was my sister, so of course I was going to help out, but I was gonna help from afar. I didn't want no parts in that mess that was about to come. Isiah was getting out of the game, which meant my mom was gonna have to find a new hustle soon.

I didn't really know Isiah and Ques, but I was proud of them dudes. Most dudes who get in the street either leave in a casket or end up jail. These dudes were getting out unscathed, and that was a blessing. They came to me asking if I could clean up some of their drug money through my trucking company. I was already looking to expand my company, so I told them I would do it. Plus, the extra twenty-five percent they offered me helped make my decision a lot easier. I told them in a couple of months is when we could get things started. Everything would be set in motion. In the meantime, they were supposed to be tying up loose ends so when it was time to handle business, there wouldn't be any mistakes.

"Demetri, dinner is ready!" Ryan called out.

"Ight."

To my surprise, Ryan called me a day ago saying she wanted to come up here to visit me. I thought the gesture was cute, but I knew there had to be more to the situation. When I presented the idea of her moving up here with me, she acted like it was the worst thing in the world. Now all of a sudden she wanted to come up here to visit me. Something was up, and I was going to find out what. I put the controller down and left out of my man cave to head to the kitchen. I had a nice three story home that I lived in by myself. The shit was lonely, which was why I was trying to get Ryan to move in with me. When she first saw the house, she fell in love with it and was talking about how she was going to decorate it.

"What took you so long to come in here? Three hours ago you were complaining about how hungry you were. Now the food is ready and you want to move slow."

"I was playing online, so I had to finish the game real quick."

"You and that damn game. I wish I would've known you were such a game head." She busied herself in the kitchen, making our plates while going on and on about my games.

"Ryan, you're wasting your breath, complaining and shit. Yeah, I play games because it gives me something to do when I'm not at work. But if you move here, then you will be my first priority, and the only thing I will be playing with is the gem that is in between your legs," I smirked. She sat a plate with two stuffed shells in front of me, then passed me a bowl of salad before sitting down across from me.

"Don't you think me moving in with you would be us moving a little too fast?"

"Show me where it says a time length for people to be dating before they can move in with each other."

"There isn't one I was just saying..."

"You were just saying what? Ryan, I'm not eighteen anymore. I'm a grown ass man that knows what he wants. I'm not here to play games with you, and from what I can see, you're not here to play games with me, so us waiting to do grown people shit makes no sense to me."

"I guess, Demetri," she sighed.

I didn't say anything, I just dug into my food. Ryan was cool as fuck and I could see a future with her, the only problem we had was that she second guessed everything that had to do with us as a couple. I know she's like that because of her ex, but I wasn't here to put up with the shit. I have told her in so many words that what we have is real and how I'm not on that fuck shit, but her ass won't believe it. She should have known I was real about my shit when I didn't leave her after she fucked that nigga. Yeah, she had an excuse, but I didn't care about that shit. She still fucked him and I stayed around, so that should have counted for something. I didn't even care when she told me she was a trained killer. All the baggage Ryan came with, I accepted without any complaints. As soon as I want her to do something that will make us stronger, she wants to give me bullshit about us moving too fast. I never lived my life on a time schedule, and I wasn't going to start now. I finished eating and cleaned my dishes, then sat back down, staring Ryan in her beautiful eyes.

"Why are you looking at me like that?" she blushed.

"Wassup with you? Why do you always make me jump through hoops?"

"No one is asking you to do anything, Demetri," she sighed as if I was annoying her.

"Stop with that sighing shit because no one cares about it. Now answer my questions."

"What questions, Demetri?"

"Don't I respect you?"

"Yes."

"Don't I make sure you're good at all times?"

"Yes."

"Don't I fuck you right?"

"Yes."

"Don't I make sweet love to every inch of your body and then do it all over again, bringing you to the highest of highs?"

"Yes, Demetri. What does this have to do with anything?"

"It has to do with everything. I treat you with all the love and respect you deserve, yet you still try to play me to the left."

"No one is trying to play you."

"Ryan, shut up because I'm talking. When you heard everything I have to say, then you can speak. For now, just listen."

"Demetri, don't talk to me like that," she sassed.

"What the hell did I just tell you? Listen to what the fuck I have to say, then you can speak. Now like I was saying, I treat you with all the love and respect that you deserve, but you still try to play me to the left. All the baggage that you got, I'm the nigga carrying it. I'm the one putting in overtime to fix what that fuck nigga messed up. I'm doing my best to show you that I'm the dude you're supposed to be with, but you keep playing me to the side. You saying we moving too fast, but I say we not moving fast enough. I want to start my life with you and it's that simple. All I want and need in my life is you. Now tell me what you need?"

"I just need someone to love me and not make me look like a fool. I want someone I can be my true self with. I just want someone to love me as much as I'm willing to love them."

"We may not be at love right now, but we are on the right path. However, we can't get to love if you're putting up all these road blocks. I know I said if you don't want to move up here then we can do the long distance thing, but I'm taking that back. I want to be with you every second, minute, and hour. I want to come home to dinner like the one you made tonight, every night. So if you not moving up here, then we might as well just end this thing right here."

I meant exactly what I said. I needed Ryan here with me, and I wasn't going to take no for an answer. If she wouldn't move up here willingly, then I would just have to kidnap her ass. I was being pushy, but I knew who and what I wanted.

"I'll move," she whispered.

"Good." I got up from my seat and walked over to where she was. I gave her a light kiss on the forehead, then walked out of the kitchen.

Knowing Ryan, she was expecting me to say something that was going to make her feel as though she didn't have anything to worry about. But I wasn't going to do that. I said all that needed to be said and she made her decision. I was a firm believer on actions speaking louder than words. I said what needed to be said, and now it was time for me to put some actions behind them words.

Chapter Twenty: Isiah

A Week Later

I was on cloud nine after leaving the doctor's office. The doctor confirmed that Harlem was indeed pregnant. She was about five weeks, and I couldn't have been happier. I was wishing for a boy, but with my luck, I would end up with a girl. Harlem was even excited about the news. I was truly blessed because everything with my family was starting to fall into place.

"We have to stop at the supermarket to get a couple of things for dinner tonight," Harlem said as we pulled away from the doctor's office.

"When you say a couple, you mean you're going to run in and come right back out, right?"

"No, I need to get some more food. You're the one that decided to have everyone over for dinner," she snapped.

"Relax, Harlem. Our family has accomplished so much that all I'm trying to do is sit us all down so we can celebrate together. Kill me for trying to do something nice."

"Yeah, you trying to do something nice, while I have to do all the cooking."

"Maybe if you told the girls you were pregnant they would want to help." I didn't understand why Harlem wanted to keep that to herself. Alani and Ryan were like her sister. I figured they would know before I did.

"They each have a lot going on within their own relationships. I didn't want to distract them from doing what they have to do."

"But y'all can sit and talk on the phone all damn day? I don't want to hear that shit. We our announcing our new addition to our family, tonight."

"That's fine with me. I don't have a problem with it. Just make sure you grab a shopping cart," she giggled, getting out of the car.

I followed behind her, making sure I grabbed the shopping cart. We walked up and down the aisle, getting everything Harlem needed for dinner. While she was running her mouth about something, my mind was elsewhere. For some strange reason, I started thinking about my mother and how she missed out on so much. Her actions didn't only hurt Alani and I, but they would also hurt our children. We grew up without a mother, and our kids would grow up without a grandmother. It was sad, but it was my reality.

"Isiah, do you not hear me talking to you?" Harlem asked, snapping her fingers in my face.

"Chill. Move your finger out my face before I snap them," I laughed.

"I was trying to ask you if you need me to buy dessert. Where was your head at?"

"In the clouds. But nah, Alani is making a blue velvet cake."

"Fat ass. That's your favorite, so I know you told her to make it," Harlem laughed.

"I can't help it. I love cake, but I love yours more," I grabbed her ass, causing her to jump a little.

"Stop it," she tried swatting my hand away, but I didn't let up.

"You gonna let me bend you over before you start cooking?"

"Nope, no nookie until I get the rock," she sassed and walked away.

I nodded my head because she was adamant about getting a ring. She thought every time she brought it up I was ignoring her, but in fact, I was planning and waiting. Yeah, I was having this dinner to get the family together to celebrate, but I was also doing it so I could give Harlem exactly what she wanted.

* * * *

"Nigga, you sure this what you want to do?" Ques asked as I showed him and Demetri the ring I got for Harlem. I got her a rare untreated oval cut ruby prong set three stone ring with half-moon shaped diamonds. The ring cost over three hundred grand, but Harlem was worth it, so it was nothing to me.

"Shit, this ring dope. You set the bar hella high for the rest of us," Demetri said.

"Alani's ass already hinting about weddings and shit after she told me she wasn't ready to be married. Her ass is just confused," Ques laughed.

"This right here is the ultimate goal. To get money, find a chick to hold you down, and then get married and have kids. Harlem is my heart, and marriage is what she wants, so that's what I'm going to give her. Plus, I want her ass to shut the fuck up about the shit. I love her, but she been getting on my nerves with this wedding shit. I'm ready to take her ass to city hall and get the shit over with."

"You know them girls would murder you if you did some shit like that," Demetri said.

"Well my nigga, it's time to turn in your player card. You ready?" Ques smiled.

"Yeah, I'm ready."

We left out the basement and walked upstairs to where the girls were. They were all in the kitchen, making their men their plates. This is why Harlem was getting this ring. She deserved it, and so did Ryan and Lani. I was sure within a year or two Demetri and Ques will be taking the same step that I'm about to take.

"Harlem, Lani, and Ryan, come in the living room real quick," I called out to them.

"Izzy, we were making the plates," Lani sassed as she walked in the living room.

"Girl, shut up. That food not going anywhere, damn," Ques told her.

"Yeah, listen to your man."

"Shut up, Izzy. Ques, mind your business," Lani giggled.

Ryan walked over to Demetri, and Harlem came to me. I pulled her to the middle of the room and got down on one knee. All the girls in the room gasped. Before I could even start to talk, Harlem started crying and nodding her head yes.

"Most of my life has been like riding a roller coaster in a pitch black cave. For so long, I was like fuck love because how could I love when my own mother didn't love me. I can't even say when you came into my life you made things better because you've been here the whole time. You have always been there for me, even when my ass was too stupid to see it. Baby, you gave me purpose. You're the reason I'm getting out the game and you didn't even know it. In a couple of months, a nigga will be legit, and it's all because of you. You're the reason I go so hard. Seeing that beautiful dimpled smile makes all the bullshit we go through worth it. You've given me a reason to succeed, a reason to better myself. You are my best friend, the one person besides my sister I can't see living without. The absolute love of my life. You're my heart, my soulmate, and to everyone else, my girlfriend. Now, I want you to be my wife. I'm not going to say will you marry me because you don't have a choice. It's me, you and the baby for life." I stood up, slipping the ring on her finger and wiping the tears away from her eyes.

"Wait, did he just say baby?" Alani screamed.

"You're pregnant?" Ryan squealed.

"Yes!" Harlem smiled, turning towards everyone.

"Oh my gosh. I'm going to be an auntie!" Ryan and Alani said at the same time.

"Congrats my nigga," Ques said, dapping me up.

"Congrats Isiah," Demetri said.

"Thank you," I smiled, holding on to my soon to be wife.

"Since everyone is making announcements, I think I should go ahead and make mine," Ryan said. We all looked at her with anticipation written on our faces. She looked up at Demetri, smiling before talking.

"As y'all know, I have been through a lot in my past relationships. I have been cheated on more times than I would like to remember, and it has changed me. The hurt and pain my ex caused me, caused me to turn into a person that was scared to pursue something new. I was scared to give myself to another man because I didn't want to go through the same hurt. Demetri came into my life at a weird time. But I'm thankful he did come into my life because he has taught me that love has no time limit. With that being said, I'm moving upstate with Demetri," she smiled.

"I'm so happy for you," Harlem said as the tears began to fall all over again.

"It's about time you made up your mind. For a second, I thought Demetri and I were gonna have to kidnap you to get you up there," Alani laughed.

"Good to know you had my back," Demetri said to Alani, causing the rest of us to laugh.

"Well I have some news that I would like to share, but first, let's get some glasses with champagne. Oh Harlem, you get sparkling apple cider," Alani laughed.

We all walked towards the kitchen, picking up a glass as Alani filled them up with champagne, and sparkling apple cider for Harlem. Alani and Ques stood before everyone, looking at each other with so much love and admiration in their eyes.

"I don't really have an announcement to make, it's more of a declaration," Alani giggled. "Ques, I just really want to say how much I love you. I know at first I was a lot to handle. I tried pushing you away because I didn't want to believe that a man could love me as strongly as you did. No matter how hard I pushed, you never went anywhere. You just pushed my ass back, and I thank you for that. I thank you for taking an interest in my baking. Not too many dudes would buy their chick a bakery, but you're not like most dudes. You really opened my heart to love. I love you and I wouldn't want to be stuck with any other asshole but you."

"Chinky, how can you be so sweet and annoying at the same time?" Ques asked, mushing her.

We all laughed as we watched them share a kiss. I would've never thought Ques would have been the one to tame Lani. But shit, she always said *All She Wanted Was Rider*, and she finally got her one.

The end!

Turn the page for a sneak peek of Jealous 2

Prologue

I turn my chin music up and I'm puffing my chest. I'm getting ready to face you, you can call me obsessed. It's not your fault that they hover I mean no disrespect. It's my right to be hellish I still get jealous. 'Cause you're too sexy, beautiful and everybody wants a taste that's why I still get jealous.

I was in the bed, trying to fall asleep when I heard my phone going off. It was playing Nick Jonas' song "Jealous", which is the ringtone I set for Messiah. I was happy that he was calling back, but pissed off at how long it took him.

"Hello?" I said, answering the phone.

"Fuck Messiah," I heard someone moan.

"Hello?" I said again. Nobody answered, but I could hear people talking in the background.

"Amara, you don't ever have to worry. I'ma always be there for you and the baby," Messiah groaned.

"Mhmmm. You love this pussy, don't you baby?"

"Hell yea."

"Tell me you love me daddy so I can cum all over this dick," Amara hissed.

"I love you baby," I heard Messiah say and I hung up the phone.

I sat in the bed, stunned at what I just heard. This bitch was really pregnant by my fucking man, and my so called man was over there telling that bitch he loved her like I didn't blow up his phone earlier. Tears started to fall down my face, but I quickly wiped them away. Messiah and Amara done fucked with the wrong one and I was going to show them just who the fuck Julani Marie Cortez was.

I got out of bed, turned on my light, and quickly found something to wear. I wanted to call Phallyn so she could ride out with me, but seeing how things went earlier, I figured this would be better if I went alone. I grabbed my .22 out my purse, and my car keys, and was headed to the door. I was moving so fast that I walked right into Cree's chest at the front door.

"Julani, where are you going in a rush, and why are you dressed like you 'bout to body someone?" Cree laughed.

"I have to go handle something," I told him, locking the door.

"Then I'm going with you," Cree said, jumping in the passenger seat.

"Cree, I don't need you coming with me. I'm a big girl. I can handle this," I told him.

"I don't know what you are trying to handle, but I do know you're pregnant with a baby that could possibly be mine."

"Thanks for reminding me," I said,

I pulled my iPod out of the glove compartment and scrolled until I found Trey Songz's "Smartphone". I hit the play button, hooked it up to the speakers in my car, and pulled off. While Trey Songz was singing about lying to his chick's face, tears were flowing down mine. I was heartbroken, but most of all, pissed off because my father and Phallyn were right. They both told me that Messiah wasn't shit, but my dumb ass didn't want to listen, and now I had to find out the hard way.

"Julani, why you listening to this depressing ass song?" Cree asked, turning it down.

"Cree, now is not the time," I told him, keeping it short.

"Let me guess, it has something to do with that other nigga. What he do now, did he call you by accident and you heard him having sex?" Cree laughed.

I looked at him with the deadliest look that I could muster up, causing his laughter to fade.

"Julani, you can't be serious. He really did that shit? Man, I already told you that nigga wasn't bout shit."

Ignoring the little comment that Cree had to say, I drove right onto the grass that was outside of Amara's house. I got out with my gun in hand and started banging on the front door. Nobody was answering the door fast enough for me. I searched their yard for a big enough rock. When I found one, I picked it up and threw it right through the window. It was around 4 in the morning and I was out here acting like a mad woman, but I honestly didn't care. If I was heartbroken, then that bitch had to be heartbroken too.

"What the fuck?" I heard Messiah yell from inside.

"Messiah, bring your dog ass out here now!" I yelled.

"Julani, what are you doing here and why the fuck you throwing shit through my windows?" Messiah yelled, coming outside.

"Fuck you and these windows. You didn't see my four missed calls?"

"You out here acting up over missed calls? Man, go ahead with that bullshit," Messiah said, dismissing me.

"Nah, I came over here to tell your bitch congratulations," I smirked.

"Oh bae, you told her the good news? Or did you get my little phone call?" Amara said, coming outside and standing next to Messiah like he was some type of prized possession. The sight of those two made me fucking sick to my stomach.

"Yea, I got your little phone call, but guess what bitch? You aren't the only one that's pregnant."

"Messiah, what the fuck is she talking about?" Amara said, hitting Messiah in the arm.

"Oh, he didn't tell you we sister wives now bitch? You ain't ever going to get rid of me!" I yelled, charging towards Amara. Messiah grabbed me and pushed me back, causing me to fall on the ground.

"My nigga, you put your hands on the wrong one," Cree said, walking towards us. This nigga was so quiet that I forgot that he was even here.

"Juju, come get your bitch boy before I lay his ass out and put him six feet under," Messiah said, getting in Cree's face.

Before I could intervene, Cree punched him in the face and the two of them started to go at it. I took a step back and just looked at all the chaos that I caused, all because I was jealous of what another woman had. I shook my head and started walking back to my car because I was truly embarrassed by the whole thing. I looked back one last time at Messiah and Cree fighting, before I got in my car and drove off.

* * * *

It has been two days since I went over to Amara's house, acting a fool. The only person that I was talking to was my father. I had both Cree and Messiah blowing my phone up, but I refused to take either one of their calls. Phallyn had stopped by my house a couple of times to check on me, but I was keeping her at arm's length too. I had too much going on in my life right now and I just didn't want to be bothered with anyone. For the past two days, I kept replaying what happened over and over in my head. I couldn't believe that I acted that way and it was all over a dude that really didn't want me to begin with.

"Julani, open the door," I heard Messiah yell outside.

I got off the living room couch and looked out the window to see Messiah standing there with a bouquet of roses. I didn't want to answer the door for him, but I still had a soft spot for him. I reluctantly opened the door and allowed him to come in.

"Messiah, what do you want?" I sighed.

"Can we at least sit and talk?"

"No, we can stay right here because you won't be staying long."

"I just want to say sorry for everything that happened the other day. I never meant for you to find out about Amara that way, and after you left, I told her that we were done for good."

"That's nice to know Messiah, but I honestly don't care."

"Julani, don't say that. We have a baby together; we can make this work," he said, caressing my cheek.

"This baby might not even be yours," I told him, pushing his hand away.

"What do you mean it might not be mine? Who the fuck baby could it be?" he yelled.

Messiah had this crazed look in his eye that made me a little nervous. I took a couple steps back, but he yanked me by the collar of my shirt.

"Messiah, please let me go," I begged.

"You let that nigga fuck you, Julani? You're trying to tell me that the baby could be his?" Messiah said, pulling a gun out from his waist.

"Messiah, what are you doing?" I asked nervously.

"Julani, I hope you don't think that I'm just going to sit back and let you carry another nigga's seed," Messiah said with tears in his eyes.

He shoved me against the wall and pointed the gun at my stomach. I closed my eyes, scared for my life, and for my unborn child's life. I heard the gun go off, and then felt the sting as the bullet ripped through me. I fell to the floor with tears in my eyes; I couldn't believe that Messiah had just shot me. People always said that jealousy was the ugliest trait. I guess I understood why now.

Chapter One

I jumped up out of my sleep with my hands roaming my body. The dream I just had of Messiah shooting me felt so real. I let out a sigh of relief when I realized it was just a dream. I couldn't lie, that dream had me nervous. I was a strong believer in dreams having a deeper meaning. That alone was my wake up call. I needed to change my life before me and my unborn child ended up dead. Since everything happened, I haven't been talking to anyone. I made sure to talk to my father every day, but other than him, I stayed to myself. Cree and Messiah have been blowing up my phone since all that shit went down. At the time, I wasn't answering because I didn't have much to say to either one of them. After having that dream, I was scared as hell to talk to Messiah, but I knew I would have to do it sooner than later.

I looked at the clock that was on my nightstand. It was only twelve in the afternoon. I needed to get up and handle my business. That dream, or should I say nightmare, put everything in perspective for me. My jealousy caused a lot of unnecessary drama that should have never taken place in the first place. I was ready to start righting my wrongs. There was no way that I was going to bring a child into this mess. I wanted to play little kid games and ended up getting myself into a grown woman situation. I wasn't proud of some of the things that I have done, but there was nothing I could do about that now.

I rolled out of bed and walked into the kitchen to get a glass of water. I thought about cooking breakfast, but nixed the idea because I started to feel nauseous. After drinking the water, I went back upstairs to jump in the shower and get dressed. My shower didn't last longer than twenty minutes. When I got out, I quickly put lotion on my body and stood in my closet, looking for something to wear. It was the middle of July, which meant it was hot and blazing out. I hated the summer so much because the heat always had me ready to walk outside naked. To me it was too hot to put on clothes and try to look cute. I grabbed a cute pink maxi dress and my Chanel sandals. Once I was dressed, I finger combed my curly hair and was out the door. The first stop was to Messiah's house. I made sure to grab my .22 before I left the house. I wasn't sure how this conversation was going to go, but I knew for a fact that if it just so happened to go left; I didn't have a problem with helping it go back right.

*****

I knocked on Messiah's door, nervous as hell. I didn't know what to expect, but I was ready for whatever. I was hoping Amara was there too because I had a couple of things to say to her too. I felt like I was knocking on his door for an eternity before the door opened. I stood there staring at the man that had me out here looking a fool. Messiah was standing in the doorway with nothing on but a pair of basketball shorts.

"Baby, who's at the door?" I heard Amara ask.

"Julani," was all Messiah said.

"Can I come in? I just want to talk. Nothing more and nothing less," I said.

He stepped to the side, allowing me to walk in. I let out the breath that I didn't realize I was holding. Amara stood there staring at me like she wanted to pounce on me.

"Look, I didn't come here for drama. I just have some things I need to get off my chest," I told her.

I walked right past her ass and sat in the living room, waiting for them to join me. Even though I came here being friendly, if Amara even thought about stepping out of line, I would switch up real quick.

I watched as Amara and Messiah sat on the couch across of me. Amara rested her hands on her belly with a smirk on her face. She really thought she was doing something, but I could honestly care less about her being pregnant.

"I came here because I realized that my behavior during the past three months has caused a lot of drama. Now, I wasn't in it alone, but I am willing to take blame for it. As the both of you know, I'm pregnant," I told them, pausing for a minute. This next part was going to be hard as hell to get out.

"Juju, you don't have to worry about anything. I'm willing and ready to be there for you and my child," Messiah spoke up.

"What you mean you're ready to be there for her?" Amara questioned real quick. "I don't mind you being there for the child, if it's even yours, but I do have problem with you being there for her."

"Amara, you don't have a say so in this. I already told you what me and you had is done. I'm just staying here to make sure everything is straight with you and the baby. Our relationship is over, and the sooner you accept it, the better."

"We are not about to have this conversation in front of this bitch," Amara spat, looking directly at me.

I laughed a little before I began to talk. "Look, there is no need for the name calling. I'm trying to be the bigger person, but if you keep coming with the insults, I will beat that ass. Now like I was saying before the two of you started going back and forth; I'm pregnant, and it may not be yours," I told Messiah, looking him directly in the eyes.

As soon as the words I said to him registered, hurt and pain were the only thing that you could see in his eyes. I didn't have intentions of hurting him, but at the same time, I needed for him to know. I clutched my purse, just in case he pulled a gun at me.

"Get the fuck out!" he barked. He had so much bass in his voice that for a minute, I thought it was my father yelling at me. I have never seen Messiah this pissed off before. I got up and started walking towards the door. I stopped in midstride because I wanted to say something. I looked back and Messiah had his face buried in his hands, while Amara rubbed his back. I figured it would be best if I just turned around and left.

I was grateful that it went a lot better than how it did in my dream, because I wasn't ready to die just yet. It was crazy because I felt the pain that Messiah was going through. His pain hit me right in my heart, but there wasn't anything that I could do about it. I wanted nothing more than to fix everything that I had broken, but it seemed as if I was just making stuff worse.

I got in my car and took a deep breath before pulling away. I got through the talk with Messiah, and now it was time to talk to Cree. Cree was a good dude that I could see myself falling for. He just so happened to come at the wrong time. I needed to talk to him too because he wanted a relationship, and I didn't think I was ready for that. Even though I had feelings for Cree, the feelings I had for Messiah were stronger. As bad as I wanted my feelings for Messiah to go away, they just weren't going to disappear that easily.

I have seen firsthand how my careless actions were hurting people that I cared about. I couldn't bring myself to be with Cree when my feelings for Messiah remained. I definitely couldn't be with him not knowing whose baby I was carrying. That alone had me feeling bad about myself. My whole young adult life I have prided myself on not being like these other fast ass girls in the streets. Shit, I even laughed at a couple of the girls that were on Maury trying to figure out who their baby daddy was. I guess you could say the joke is on me now because I was in the same boat as them. Pregnant and not knowing which dude fathered my baby.

Contact Me

Website: Kellzkinc.com

Facebook: Kellz Kimberly

Instagram: Kellzkimberlyxoxo

Snapchat: Kellzkayy

CPSIA information can be obtained
at www.ICGtesting.com
Printed in the USA
LVHW091336190220
647479LV00001BA/123